THE MAGE THINKS
SOME SAGE THOUGHTS

There is talk in some learned circles of our major cities about whether or not satyrs, centaurs, griffins and certain other fantastic beasts really exist, or are only the product of the popular imagination. As a wizard, I, of course, tend to side with the satyrs, centaurs, and griffins, especially when these beasts begin to doubt the existence of any learned circles in our major cities.

— from THE TEACHINGS OF EBENEZUM,
Volume XXXVI

"A delight for all fans of funny fantasy!"
—Will Shetterly, author of
Cats Have No Lord

"Devastating send-ups of all the stock props . . . dragons and damsels in distress, eternal champions, swords and sausage, unicorns, virgins and other improbable critters."
—Marvin Kaye, author of
The Amorous Umbrella

Ace Fantasy books by Craig Shaw Gardner

A MALADY OF MAGICKS
A MULTITUDE OF MONSTERS

A MULTITUDE OF MONSTERS

Craig Shaw Gardner

ACE FANTASY BOOKS
NEW YORK

This book is an Ace Fantasy original edition,
and has never been previously published.

A MULTITUDE OF MONSTERS

An Ace Fantasy Book/published by arrangement with
the author

PRINTING HISTORY
Ace Fantasy edition / September 1986

ISBN: 0-441-54523-8

Ace Fantasy Books are published by The Berkley Publishing Group,
200 Madison Avenue, New York, N.Y. 10016.
PRINTED IN THE UNITED STATES OF AMERICA

**This one's for
Merrilee, also without whom . . .**

ONE

When traveling, the sages say, one must always be prepared to accept local customs. Yet there are areas of this very kingdom where one might find it customary to tax a wizard into poverty; to insist a wizard should not be paid, for magic exists only for the common good; or even to tar and feather a wizard unsuccessful at his task. Contrary to the sages, when one is traveling in these areas, one should be prepared to avoid local customs altogether.

—*THE TEACHINGS OF EBENEZUM,*
                    VOLUME VI

I had walked through dark forests before, but never one as dark as this. The massive trees we passed between rose high above our heads, their branches meeting hundreds of feet in the air to weave a green blanket above us. They let so little light to the forest floor that half the day we seemed to march through evening, and the rest of the day was blackest night.

I had walked through treacherous undergrowth before, but none more treacherous than this. Despite the fact that little light seeped through the leaves above, the ground about our feet was littered with bushes, low things with pale leaves that looked as if they thrived on darkness rather than light. The leaves held sharp edges as well, and hid sharper brambles beneath that would stick to your leggings, and draw blood if you touched them.

I had walked through chill climates before, but none where the cold seeped right through muscle and bone the way it did here. Not only did the leaves above banish sunlight, but also any memory of warmth that the sun might bring. I felt that the blood on my bramble-sore fingers might freeze if the temperature were to descend the slightest degree.

My master, the wizard Ebenezum, once the greatest mage in all the Western Kingdoms, turned to regard the rest of our procession. He stretched his arms out beyond the sleeves of his wizardly robes, black silk tastefully inlaid with silver moons and stars, a bit soiled and torn from the rigors of our trip, perhaps, but still the sign of a serious sorcerer. He yawned and scratched at his full white beard.

"Oh, what a bracing morning," the wizard remarked.

"Doom!" a voice called behind me. Without turning, I could tell it was the warrior Hendrek, his grip tight about the sack that held his doomed warclub, Head-basher. Hendrek, it appeared, felt much the same as I.

"Yztwwrfj!" added yet another voice, this one belonging to the demon Snarks, so deeply clothed in layer upon layer of robe that anything he said was completely indecipherable. Still, did I sense disquiet in the tone of his voice?

"Oh, come now." The wizard stroked his mustache

contemplatively. " 'Tis not as bad as all that. We have not had to deal with a demon attack for well over two days. We are making good time through this forest; in a few more days we shall reach the Inland Sea. And on the other side of that sea lies Vushta!"

Vushta? I must admit, even in that gloomy forest, the name alone cheered my spirits. Vushta, city of a thousand forbidden delights, a place where, were he not the soul of caution, a man might go mad with myriad desires. Vushta, where a young lad such as myself had to be doubly careful, lest he be dragged unwillingly to one of the city's fabled pleasure palaces, and there forced, no matter how he might protest—

An explosion disturbed my thoughts.

"Eh?" the wizard remarked. "Well, perhaps I was mistaken."

"Doom!" Hendrek repeated. The large warrior stepped to my side. His whole body quivered with anticipation; a fearsome sight to see, for he was almost as wide as he was tall. His hand clutched convulsively at the bag that contained his enchanted weapon. "We are in the presence of some dread magic!"

I glanced up, wondering if I should correct him. I knew, for the moment at least, that Hendrek was wrong. There was no great magic here yet. My master had not sneezed.

As I have said, Ebenezum was once the greatest wizard in all the Western Kingdoms. And really, he was still a mage without peer, save for one problem. A few scant months ago, due to a small error on his part, the wizard found himself fighting for his life with Guxx Unfufadoo, one of the most powerful demons the Netherhells has ever seen. Ebenezum defeated the demon, and banished it to the Netherhells once again, but his battle was not without its cost. From that day forward, should he even be in the presence of magic, the wizard would begin to sneeze violently and uncontrollably.

Now, a malady of this sort might defeat many a lesser wizard. But not Ebenezum! He continued to ply his trade, using his affliction to sniff out sorcery wherever it might lurk, while at the same time seeking a cure among his learned tomes. At last, however, even a wizard as great as Ebenezum had to admit he could not cure his malady alone. He would have to seek outside assistance, even though he might have to travel to far and fabled Vushta, city of a thousand forbidden delights, before he might find another wizard with skill sufficient for this enormous task.

So to Vushta we journeyed. And as we journeyed we encountered demons and dragons, giants and ghosts, trolls and enchanted chickens! There was sorcery everywhere we turned. Far too much sorcery.

It was when we were staying in a hermit's very large and palatial hovel that we learned the truth; only as we were attacked again by Guxx Unfufadoo, the very demon that caused my master's malady! The Netherhells, not content with an occasional bit of demonic intervention, had mounted a campaign to take over the surface world as well and turn it into an extension of their foul domain!

Ebenezum and I, with the help of many others, managed to win that first battle. But we knew it was only the beginning of the war. Now, it was even more imperative that we reach Vushta and its College of Wizards. The future of the whole world was at stake!

Since then, we had redoubled our endeavors to complete our journey, aided by our two companions, Snarks and Hendrek. But even in our daily travels, we had to observe extreme caution. Besides an occasional attack by human assassins, hired by a ruler Ebenezum had managed to slightly offend some time ago, we were constantly being set upon by demons and demonic magic, and 'twas only through our combined efforts that we managed to survive.

There was another explosion, much closer this time. The earth shook at our feet.

"Doom!" the large warrior repeated. "The demons attack again!"

"No, no, good Hendrek," my master corrected. " 'Tis not demons, yet. As least not in any force. My nose would not be able to withstand such an assault."

The wizard stepped hastily back, drawing up his robes to cover his lower face. With the third explosion, Hendrek had drawn Headbasher from its protective sack.

"Doom!" Hendrek swung the warclub above his head so quickly that the air screamed with its passing. Headbasher was an enchanted club, and when the large warrior held it in his hands, he became like a man possessed. But Headbasher's magic was a curse as well, for Hendrek had obtained the club from the demon Brax, who neglected to inform the warrior as to the exact terms of sale. To his everlasting horror, Hendrek soon learned that Headbasher was a club no man could own, but could only rent!

Snarks had pulled his sickly green demonic head free of his concealing robes. He stood next to Hendrek, staring at the site of the last explosion.

"The wizard is right," Snarks hissed. "No demon has done this. It is something far worse!"

There was an explosion by Snarks's right foot. The demon screamed.

"Oh, excuse me!" a small voice exclaimed. "Pardon, pardon, pardon!" A very diminutive fellow dressed all in brown stood in our midst. He brushed distractedly at his sleeves. "I don't quite have that trick down yet. I'm very close, though!"

Hendrek squinted in the newcomer's direction. " 'Tis some kind of Fairy. . . ."

"What!" The little man glared at the large warrior. "I am nothing of the kind! The very idea!" He took a deep breath, drawing himself up to his full height (just under a foot and a half). "Gentlemen, I am a Brownie!"

"Brownie?" Snarks murmured. The look of distaste on his countenance turned to one of pure horror. "Brownie?"

Hendrek smiled at the Brownie. "Well, little man, 'twas a natural mistake. You know how everyone talks about Fairies and Brownies."

"Fairies and Brownies! Fairies and Brownies!" The little man stamped his feet in indignation. "It's never Brownies and Fairies, no, no, no, never the other way around! Well, we Brownies have had enough! We're not going to take it anymore!"

"Indeed," Ebenezum said behind the folds of his robe. "Would it be impolite to ask just what you were not going to take?"

The little fellow shook his head sadly. " 'Tis a longstanding truth that Brownies have always been taken for granted. Well, it's partially our fault, I'll be the first to admit that. My ancestors did a lot of hiding from you big folks, and it's always been the Brownie Way to get most of our work done after dark. Well, believe me, the days of the invisible Brownies are over! From now on, when we do good deeds, you'll darn well see them. Up with Brownies!"

Snarks shuddered, clearly appalled by the very thought. I studied our green companion with some concern. With his thorough knowledge of the Netherhells, Snarks had been of invaluable assistance in our battles with demonic forces. Could he perhaps sense something sinister in this small man's speech?

In a whisper, I asked the demon what was wrong.

Snarks looked at me, misery in his eyes. If anything, his sickly green complexion was even more sickly and more green than usual.

"You know," he whispered hoarsely, "that I have been banished from the Netherhells, for, due to demonic politicians scaring my mother while I was in infancy, I can speak nothing but the truth. And, for the most part, I have come to accept my lot in life—forced to wander the surface world, the enemy of my kin and kind, most of whom would kill me on sight. And still . . . and still . . ."

Snarks choked back a ragged sob. "It is just too much! I may have been driven from the Netherhells . . . but I still have some standards. He's so, so . . ." Snarks gagged. "So . . . CUTE!"

I looked back at the Brownie. I could see the demon's point. There was something about that foot-and-a-half high fellow, jumping up and down and saying positive things about Browniedom, that was absolutely nauseating.

"Where are the Fairies now, let me ask you that?" the little man was saying now. "You think they don't know about the plans that the Netherhells have for these parts? No, no, no, those Fairies know everything about every demon that's ever set foot in the realm! But do they do anything about it? No, not the Fairies! They're too frightened! They go into hiding! Well, now it's the Brownies' time. We're not going to go into hiding again. We're going to wait right here, and show the demons and everybody that the Brownies have come to stay! Fairies and Brownies, indeed!''

"Indeed," Ebenezum replied. "Very commendable."

"In fact," the Brownie beamed, "that's the reason
I've come. There was this young lady I just met, back in
the forest a bit, who had a very important message for
you!''

"Young lady?" I asked.

"Yes, yes, her name began with an *N* I think. Well,
an *N* or an *M*." The Brownie shook his head. "There's
something to be said for that mode of transportation.
It's certainly good if you're in a hurry, but I must say
those explosions shake one up a bit."

"An *N*?" I queried. "Was the woman's name
Norei?" Could it be true? Was my true love trying to
find us? Perhaps, dare I hope, she could not exist
another minute without me?

"It might have been an *S*. Excuse me. It's this ringing
in my ears, you know. But it's one of those for sure,
either an *M* or an *N*, or possibly an *S*. It's got to be one
of those, I'm quite certain of that."

Couldn't this Brownie be more specific? It had to be
Norei! Didn't it? Perhaps, I thought, the message she
had for us would give me some clue.

"What did she have to say?" I demanded. "Did she
mention Ebenezum?" For a second, my voice caught in
my throat. "Did she say anything about . . . Wuntvor?"

"Well, she may have used one of those names. Yes, I
think she did. Now, what *did* her name start with?"

"I see." This was obviously all too much for my
master. He strode forward, his great, bushy eyebrows
knitted with concern. I must admit, I was relieved to see
the wizard take a truly active role in this interrogation.
His sorcerous wiles could get to the bottom of anything.
Magic or no magic, he'd get an answer from this forest
spirit.

"What did the young woman tell you?" He sneezed briefly, then turned away to blow his nose.

"Well, let's see," the Brownie said. "You know, I can't tell you just now. It's that name thing. Funny how something small like that can just get in your way, but when I get bothered like that—was it an *M*?"

The wizard stepped forward to try again. "Can you find out what the young woman told you?" He sneezed twice this time.

"Well, I could go back and ask her her name. I bet it'll all come back to me then. You've got to give me a chance here. Us Brownies are going to take a more active role in this world than ever before. We're really set on doing that. But, we're a little new at it. You've got to give us a little time to grow. I promise I won't let you down. This is our Brownie Pledge: We'll keep on doing it until we get it right."

Ebenezum managed only one word before the sneezing fit took him: "Go!"

"Oh. Pardon me. Yes, I guess I'd better. Well, remember, Brownies do it better!"

He closed his eyes and stamped his feet.

Snarks yelped as the air exploded at his feet.

The Brownie smiled weakly. "Sorry. Still having a little trouble finding the range." He frowned. "Whatever that young woman had to say, I know it was important. What was it? Oh yes, a matter of life and death. That's what she said. Life and death. Or was it life *or* death?"

There was another explosion. This time, the Brownie was gone.

TWO

There are as many styles of magic as there are magicians. While much of magic is gaudy, noisy, and easily appreciated by the masses, it goes without saying that some of the finest sorcery is also the most subtle; small, delicate changes in the fabric of being that often can only be discerned by another wizard's practiced eye. Occasionally, even a wizard as learned as myself will experience a twinge of regret that I have not yet conquered some of the most delicate aspects of my art; that, for example, I have not learned the Eastern finger magic, where, by the turn of a knuckle, the mage may make the flowers sing. And perhaps some day my fingers might learn that art, on the day they become tired from constantly carrying about the large amounts of gold I receive for performing the more gaudy and noisy magic that pays so well.

—THE TEACHINGS OF EBENEZUM,
VOLUME VII

"Norei!"

The word escaped my lips as the Brownie disappeared. Norei! The greatest love of my life. How could I describe her? Her face, her hair, her skin, the way she smiled? No, mere words could not do justice to the way I felt about her. Norei! And if the Brownie could be trusted, she was coming to join me!

Some would say we were too young to be so in love. But appearances are often deceiving. I will admit that there were times, in my earlier life, when I thought I was in love and it was not so. There was a certain rich farmer's daughter, and another girl, who, instead of remaining with me, decided to pursue a career in show business with a singing dragon, and, now that I think of it, perhaps five or six others. But you must understand that it was only through meeting Norei that I discovered true, true love. Yes, it was only through knowing Norei that I discovered that everything before was nothing more than youthful infatuation.

Now, though, my life was different. I was a man of the world, on my way to Vushta, city of a thousand forbidden delights. Even a magician's apprentice grows quickly on a journey such as this. When traveling to Vushta, one had to be ready for anything.

"I do not trust the Brownie."

I glanced up. The demon Snarks had moved to my side as I stood lost in thought. He had tossed back his hood so that his whole green scaled head was exposed, horns and all. His large, well-fanged mouth was turned downward into one of the most miserable-looking grimaces I had ever seen.

"Why, friend Snarks," I inquired, "what could a Brownie do that might cause us harm?"

"The very point!" the demon cried. His red eyes peered intently into my own. "Just what do Brownies do? Very little, as far as I can tell. Oh, there's this piffle about them fixing shoes in the middle of the night. Sounds like a cheap way for shoemakers to gain some unwarranted sales! Enchanted Brownie shoes, phfahh! I wouldn't be surprised if the shoemakers and the Brownies were in this together! I tell you, Brownies are just too quiet for their own good!'' Snarks kicked a me-dium-sized rock out of the path before us. The demon glowered with an intensity only possible for one raised in the Netherhells.

"Doom!" The great warrior Hendrek moved to my other side. "There was something about that Brownie, then? 'Tis true, no one should look that cheerful with-out good reason." Hendrek nervously fingered the sack that held Headbasher. He glowered with an intensity only possible for one possessed by an enchanted war-club.

I glanced back and forth between my two compan-ions. How they had changed in our two weeks of travel-ing together! When first they met, I was afraid each would tear the other limb from limb. Hendrek had gained his cursed warclub through demons, and thus had no great love of the species. And Snarks, in his de-sire to tell all the truth all the time, seemed to take par-ticular delight in informing the very large warrior as to the efficiency of certain diet and exercise programs. But Snarks had been indispensable in his knowledge of de-monic strategy during our recent skirmishes with the Netherhells, and Hendrek was no less useful with his flashing warclub, Headbasher. The two, at last, realized that they needed each other. Now, while they were still not the best of friends, they did manage to speak occa-sionally, and I no longer feared the imminent murder of one at the hands of the other.

There was a loud harummph from the path before us.

"If you wish to continue your private discussion," the wizard remarked, "the least you might do is march at the same time. We have much ground to cover before this half-light fails us." Ebenezum glowered with an intensity only possible for a great mage cut off from his art.

I realized then that my master was feeling the ardours of our journey as much as the rest of us. There was exhaustion in his voice, and creases about his beard that I hadn't seen before. My master, the wizard Ebenezum, seemed to handle the march, and the occasional battle that came with it, with such aplomb that I sometimes forgot that he, too, could grow weary. He was unable to approach us any closer, for, if the wizard should close upon Snarks without the demon's protective hood, or if the mage should be in the vicinity of Headbasher when the club was drawn from its sack, the great Ebenezum would be totally lost to a sneezing attack. As I thought about it, I realized it could do him no good to be further cut off from conversation with his fellows due to the severity of his malady. I told him of our concerns.

"Indeed." The wizard stroked his beard thoughtfully. " 'Tis but one way to see if the Brownie is playing us true or false. We must make our own magic to contact the young witch!"

Magic! Alas, at that point in my young career, I knew far too little about it. During the time of my early apprenticeship, back in the Western Woods, Ebenezum had been too busy to instruct me in much more than sweeping and bucket carrying. Then, with the arrival of his malady, and our subsequent discovery of the fiendish plots of the Netherhells, things became far more hectic. Well, we needed new magic, and Ebenezum suggested we try some. I listened attentively. I may have been ignorant of spells, but surely my eagerness would more than make up for any knowledge I lacked.

"Indeed," Ebenezum remarked, noting my extreme attention with a single, raised eyebrow. "I suggest a communication spell. Very effective and very simple. Wuntvor should be able to master it in no time."

Holding his nose delicately, the wizard pulled me aside.

"Wuntvor." My master spoke softly, but with great feeling. "I believe we have come to a turning point in our journeys. Once we left Heemat's behind, we left civilization as well. We will not see another town before the edge of the Inland Sea." He paused a moment to stroke his long white mustache. "I sense some dissent between our companions. Both have proved their worth on this journey, as I am sure they will continue to do. But both will be of much more worth if we give them leadership. And magic is what makes us leaders. As we've seen, I can still manage a spell or two under duress, but it takes far too much out of me. And we need more than that. Simple spells, everyday things to keep our spirits up. This, Wunt, is where you can be invaluable."

The wizard coughed discreetly. "I know I have been remiss in the past in teaching you your craft. I apologize for that. You know about the circumstances. Now, though, I must teach you the spells that will serve us from day to day. Whatever happens, we must continue to appear to be in control of our situation here."

So he had heard us after all. I agreed with him totally. We would only be able to succeed if we kept our spirits up. It was the one way Hendrek and Snarks would make it through. He did not have to mention how much he and I needed it as well.

"Wuntvor," my master intoned. "I remember a spell that you should have no trouble with at all." He clapped me on the shoulder. "We have need of the contents of your pack."

Quickly, I removed the heavy burden from my back. When we had left from our home in the Western Kingdoms, Ebenezum had brought what learned tomes and magical paraphernalia we might have use of on our journeys. As his apprentice, it was of course my duty to carry these important belongings, especially since, as my master had so often told me, a wizard should keep his hands free for quick conjuring and his mind free for sorcerous conjecture. Heavy as these items were, they had already proved indispensable on a number of occasions, and I had begun to think of the weighty pack as almost a part of me, especially since I could depend on my stout oak staff to help support the weight when the going got rough, and to keep me from pitching forward when we traveled downhill.

Ebenezum briefly outlined his plan and, after a moment's rummaging through the crowded sack, I found just what the wizard requested: the Spring issue of *Conjurer's Quarterly*. I could tell at a glance that it was just what we wanted, for, in the bottom right-hand corner of the bright yellow cover, just below the painting of the attractive, smiling witch, were the words, printed in an even brighter red, *Five Simple Spells Even Your Apprentice Can Master*. This was for me! I quickly turned to the appropriate page.

And there it was, right after "Basic Cleaning Spell" and just before "Basic Romance Spell" (I'd have to come back to that one later), "Basic Communication Spell: Communicate Better Through Visual Aids!"

The wizard frowned thoughtfully in my direction. "So Wuntvor. Do you think you are up to it?"

I nodded eagerly. "Yes, master. We will speak with Norei in no time!" The spell was little more than a series of pictures. If using this spell meant I could speak with my beloved, I knew I would not fail!

"Good, 'prentice." The wizard scratched thoughtfully beneath his cap. "I shall be nearby if you require advice. Or at least as nearby as I deem safe." My master quietly moved a few paces away.

I returned my attention to the learned periodical.

"Think of magical thoughts as you might think of birds," the instructions began. "Your thoughts may fly through the air as birds may fly, and they may land miles and miles from that point at which they began their flight. To best use this spell, you must picture yourself as a bird in flight, a noble hawk, perhaps, which brings tidings of great import, or a gentle dove, bearing a message of love."

Beneath these words were a series of drawings: a hawk in flight; a swan upon a lake; a dove carrying a rose in its beak. "Look at one of these images, or look at a real bird in flight, and concentrate. Your thoughts are that bird, flying to a perch of your choosing. But remember, concentration is the key! Let nothing distract you—"

"Doom!"

Hendrek's cry startled me from my reading. Then Ebenezum sneezed, and I lost my place completely.

A cloud of sickly yellow smoke was congealing a few feet away from the large warrior. Hendrek's club was free of its restraining sack. Snarks had thrown back his hood, his head now free to see and speak the truth. We needed all our wits about us now.

"Easy payments!" the just-materialized demon cried.

"Along with your hellishly small fine print!" Snarks hissed back.

"So, you are still here, traitor?" The newly materialized demon continued to smile broadly as it ducked a blow from Headbasher. It brushed the dust from its orange-and-green checkerboard costume, and puffed on a foul-smelling cigar. Brax, for it was the Salesdemon, pointed at Hendrek. "Of course, my most honored client here should not believe a single word this despicable demon has to say. After all, how can you trust someone with his origins?"

"They are your origins as well, merchant Brax!" Snarks cried.

"See what I mean?" Brax flicked some cigar ash into Snarks's robes. "This creature has absolutely no sales awareness." The salesdemon sighed melodramatically. "Who would have thought someone raised in the Netherhells could be so dull, pedantic and boring."

"Me, dull? Me, boring?" Snarks retorted. "Only if the truth is boring!"

"Ah, so we at least agree on that," Brax rapidly replied. "Which brings me to the reason for my visit. I trust, Hendrek, you have so far been satisfied with the performance of your enchanted weapon?"

Headbasher crashed noisily against the rocks where, only a moment before, Brax had stood.

"Doom!" the larger warrior intoned.

I realized with a start that someone was tugging on my robes. I looked about to see my master, enveloped in his robes, doing his best not to sneeze.

"Wuntvor," he managed. He nodded his head towards a place somewhat farther up the path.

I rapidly followed my master to the point he had indicated. Ebenezum sneezed once, then blew his nose voluminously on a corner of his sleeve.

"Good," the wizard remarked, once he had caught his breath. "We must be wary of further distractions. Did it not cross your mind, Wuntvor, that the coming of the demon Brax might be the very event Norei has attempted to warn us about?''

I looked back in horror at Brax, who was offering the warrior a line of warclub accessories which, the demon assured Hendrek, ''would make Headbasher even better!'' Actually, the wizard's surmise had not crossed my mind for an instant. Brax was always coming around to annoy Hendrek, and to demand that the warrior do this or that foul deed in partial payment for the enchanted club. It was one of the things I had come to depend on in our travels. But then, what more fiendish plot could there be than something from the Netherhells that we had grown to expect?

''Yes!'' Brax shouted as he once again dodged Headbasher. ''You'd be able to crush me easily if you had a Netherhells Extendoclub (patent pending) attached to your weapon! Here's how the little marvel works—''

''Therefore,'' the wizard continued, drawing my attention back to the matter at hand, ''it is imperative that we contact Norei without further delay. Have you sufficiently studied the spell?''

I told my master I would have it in a minute. I found my place again in the learned periodical. It did seem simple enough. Essentially, you had to envision yourself as a bird. Well, I had once been turned into a bird by a spell that had gone the slightest bit wrong. True, the bird had been a chicken, and chickens aren't generally known for their powers of flight, but that was a minor quibble. I remembered the experience very well, and, in fact, would on occasion still get an overwhelming urge to eat dried seed corn. I would just have to use my imagination and transfer my experience to a bird with a better wingspan.

After that, one merely had to picture that person

with whom one desired to communicate, recite a simple
phrase or two, and the spell was complete. As the
learned article said, "Concentration is the key." It
didn't seem like any problem at all.

I looked at the picture of the hawk. That would be
nice. I would become the noble hawk, and fly to my
beloved.

"Shoddy workmanship?" Brax screamed. "What do
you mean, shoddy workmanship?"

"Admit it!" Snarks retorted. "You remember those
singing swords that couldn't carry a tune!"

"Well, yes, that was a problem," Brax admitted. "I
could only sell them to clients who were tone deaf."

"And what about those love potions that attracted in-
sects?" Snarks cried triumphantly. "Imagine how upset
people got, surrounded by hordes of amorous mos-
quitoes?"

"Quality control is not my department!" Brax cried,
clearly on the defensive. "Besides, I deal exclusively
with used weapons. If you have a complaint about that,
you have to direct it to Potion Control! They're open, I
think, every third Tuesday. . . ."

It was no use. I simply couldn't concentrate on being
a noble hawk with all this racket. I decided I would
imagine myself as a sleek, white dove instead. How romantic, to visit my true love in the image of a dove!

"Doom!" Hendrek's warclub came crashing down
where Brax had been.

"Wuntvor," my master whispered. "Hurry! We
must find the true reason for Brax's arrival!"

The wizard had a point. "Concentration is the key."
Somehow, though, I couldn't quite get a picture of a
dove firmly in my mind.

"Good Hendrek!" Brax cried as the demon leapt
above a low swing of Headbasher. "You misunderstand

me! I have only your best interests at heart!"

"Foul fiend—," Hendrek began to bellow, but then he hesitated. "Yes, you do often arrive just before a battle. Why do you always warn us?"

Brax's smile grew even broader. "Simply good business practices, friend Hendrek. We have to make sure you remain alive until we see sufficient return on our investment. How would we demons ever get paid if we didn't warn people?"

"Doom!" Hendrek cried, Headbasher once again flying through the air. "I will never fulfill your hellish contracts!"

"Oh come now. It's not as difficult as all that." Brax waved its cigar at Snarks. "What say, as the first payment, you eliminate a certain green and sickly fellow in a hood? Just reach out with your weapon, and no one will ever tell you to diet again!"

"Doom! Doom! Doom!" Hendrek attacked Brax with redoubled fury.

"Listen—urk—" Brax paused to somersault out of the way. "Like I said, good Hendrek, you're an investment. Eeps! A little close there. Just think of us—urk—as having a long and endearing friendship. Like we always say in the Netherhells, 'No money down, a lifetime to pay.' "

"Wuntvor!" Ebenezum whispered, again urgently.

Yes, yes, my master was right! I could no longer let the drama at the other end of the clearing distract me. I had to succeed, for my master, for Norei! But images of hawks and doves flitted away every time the noise level rose. Somehow, I needed to clearly see a bird in my mind's eye.

The doomed warclub, Headbasher, struck a tree with a resounding thump. A bird flew from an upper branch with a harsh cry of protest. A bird! It was truly a sign. I

concentrated on the fowl's deep brown feathers. I
would use this bird's image, common and workmanlike,
to be my messenger. What need had I for distant hawk
and dove? The sturdy grackle would be my guide!

Quickly, I set my mind to its task. The wizard ex-
horted me one final time to gain Norei's message. I nodded, reciting the short, mystic spell. "Concentration is
the key!" Fly thoughts! Fly like a grackle, brown wings
beating against the air. Fly to my beloved Norei!

Norei! I saw her then, far below me, as if I did fly
through the air. Her hair was a brilliant red in the mid-
day sun. She looked up as I approached, her beautiful
green eyes filled with wonder.

"Wuntvor?" Her perfect lips spoke my name.

She spoke my name! All thoughts of grackles fled my
head. I blinked. Ebenezum stood before me, hands
covering his nose. Norei was gone!

"Well, Wuntvor?" Ebenezum asked.

"Don't say I didn't warn you!" Brax called and
waved. "Don't worry! You've got a friend in Brax.
After all, I've got my investment to worry about! I'll be
seeing you!"

The demon popped out of existence.

A terrible cry rose all about us. We were in the midst
of a demon attack!

THREE

In magic, as in all true professions, there are rules by which you must play. At least, you must play by them until such time as you can get away with something else.

—*THE TEACHINGS OF EBENEZUM,*
VOLUME I (PREFACE)

There was an explosion at my feet.

"Pardon me," a small voice said. "We Brownies like to arrive with a bang! I have good news for you!" The fellow's little eyes gazed about in amazement. "My, my, what's going on here?"

What was going on here was that, once again, all of the Netherhells had broken loose. I suppose that, after a time, one should get used to this sort of thing. Heaven knows we had seen enough demon attacks in the last few days. Somehow, though, there was something about being attacked by a large number of creatures equipped with tearing claws and rending fangs that never lost its ability to startle.

"Bllrorowr!"

The dark, hairy thing attacked me again. I should never have looked at the Brownie. I swung my stout oak staff at the place where the thing's face should be. The fiend had too much hair for me to discern most of its facial features. The only thing I was able to see were far too many teeth.

The hairy thing backed away with a scream. I must have hit something vital! I wished I knew what it was so I could do it again. I risked a moment to see how my fellows were faring.

Snarks was caught up in battle with a purple mass of muscle, while Hendrek fought off a dozen creatures with the thwacking Headbasher. Ebenezum was sneezing somewhere deep within his robes, but he was safe for the moment. We seemed to be keeping this horde of fiends at bay. I guessed that, like anything else, all this practice was sharpening our skills at fighting the Netherhells! I swung my stout oak staff at the hairy thing once again. The creature leapt back in alarm. Take that, I thought, foul fiends! The worst hordes of the Netherhells don't stand a chance against Ebenezum's noble band!

A large, slavering thing leapt straight for the Brownie.

"Oh, is that all?" the Brownie remarked. The small fellow winked three times as he did a small dance.

The large, slavering thing disappeared.

"How did you do that?" I said with some astonishment.

The Brownie glanced at his feet. "I believe it's called the fox trot." He winked in my direction. "That, of course, combined with Brownie Power!"

"Doom!" Hendrek cried, bonking the only demon that still faced him.

"Urk!" the demon cried as it disappeared. The

demon confronting Snarks shrieked and disappeared as well. I realized then all the demons had vanished.

"Pretty nifty, huh?" The Brownie was all smiles.

"Don't give the little fellow too much credit," Snarks remarked. "That was a simple Netherhells' Multiplication Spell. It is child's play to reverse something like that."

The smile vanished from the Brownie's face. "That's right, belittle us. I mean, we are called the little people, after all. We're short, why should anyone pay any attention to us?"

"My thoughts exactly," Snarks agreed. "And now that we've gotten this fellow out of the way, perhaps we can get about our business?"

"Out of the way?" the Brownie shouted. "Let's see you try to put Brownie magic out of the way!" The little man began to dance furiously.

"Doom!" Headbasher came crashing down in the space between Snarks and the Brownie. Hendrek glowered darkly at the others.

"We fight demons," the large warrior asserted. "We do not fight among ourselves."

"And what do you mean?" I interjected. "What's a Netherhells' Multiplication Spell?"

"Oh, it's a typically shoddy piece of Netherhells chicanery," the Brownie remarked casually. "They use it when they don't have enough demons to go around. It's purely a last-chance diversionary spell."

"You mean," I asked, "that we weren't attacked by a horde of demons?"

"Only if you define horde as any group containing two or more," the Brownie replied.

I tapped my stout oak staff on the ground in disbelief. I remembered the feel of the weapon in my hands as it whistled through the air toward the hairy thing, the satisfaction as the creatures leapt away in fear. We could best anything the Netherhells sent against us!

"That's all that were there?" I asked. "Two?"

"Yes," the Brownie replied cheerfully. "Those spells can keep you occupied for hours. Then they vanish. By that time they've kept you away from whatever goal you've been trying to reach until it's far too late. Or maybe they've just kept you standing in one place long enough for the real nasty stuff to arrive!"

"I could have told you that!" Snarks cut in. "I know all about that sort of thing! And I can tell a demon from a phantom as well as the next magical creature!"

"Yes," the Brownie replied. "But did you?"

"Listen, short stuff!" Snarks was shouting now. "I would have if you hadn't been doing all this grandstanding. It's getting so an honest demon can't get a word in edgewise. Why don't you talk about things you know about, like making shoes?"

"There we go again!" the little fellow cried. "Brownie stereotyping! I'll have you know—"

"Doom!"

Headbasher crashed between the two again.

"What did I tell you two about arguing?"

"Arguing?" Snarks shrugged his cloaked shoulders. "Why, friend Hendrek, 'tis nothing more here than a simple difference of opinion, a discussion of definitions, if you will. But arguing?" Snarks patted Headbasher gently.

"Doom," Hendrek replied somewhat more gently. "We must repair to Vushta with all speed. Our very lives depend on it."

Ebenezum called to us from some distance away. "The warrior is right. I, too, discerned the deception on the part of the Netherhells, but was unfortunately too incapacitated to act. Whatever the reason for the multiplication spell, it bodes ill. Quickly Wuntvor, you must tell us. What news did you gain from Norei?"

Norei! In the ensuing madness, I had quite forgotten my one, shining moment of contact. She had spoken my name! Of course, my concentration had slipped a bit in that moment. Whose would not have? Now, how best to explain it to the wizard . . .

Norei! Of course—the Brownie had come back! He had the message!

"Quickly, small fellow!" I cried to the Brownie. "Tell us what words the woman had for us!"

"What?" The Brownie started, as if the very idea of a message was news to him. He scratched his tiny head. "Oh, yes. The message. I remembered the young woman's name! It was Norei!" The Brownie nodded and smiled, obviously waiting for approval.

Norei! My beloved's name came close to dissolving my resolve. But no! I must find out from the Brownie what I had failed to ask of her.

"Indeed," I said, emulating my master. "We are very glad you now know the young woman's name. Would you please give us the message as well?"

"Message? Oh, yes." The Brownie coughed. "The message. Oh dear. My, my. I knew I'd forgotten something."

"See?" Snarks cried triumphantly. "What did I tell you? Brownies! Get them away from their shoelaces—"

"Sir!" the Brownie said sharply. "We Brownies will not be intimidated. We make shoes, yes, but we make very good shoes. Remember sir, the Brownie Creed: We are short, but we are many."

Snarks shivered. "Thousands of tiny shoemakers, stretching to the horizon—" The demon paused as he watched Hendrek nervously finger Headbasher. He turned back to the Brownie. "Well, perhaps I am snapping at you too soon. Anything is possible with a few years of practice."

The Brownie held up his hands. "All right, all right. I admit that my performance has been just a tad spotty up to now. Like I said, we Brownies are a little new to public performance. I tell you what. There's none of those wimp Fairies around, right? Well, take my word for it, those guys go into hiding when there's a thunderstorm. Something like this and you'd have better luck finding a tax collector on refund day. See? I do know the ways of mortals."

The Brownie leapt to a nearby tree stump to give himself some height. "I hearby make a pledge!" His tiny fist pounded his tiny chest. "We all know what Fairies are good for. You know, the three wishes bit? Well, I'm here to show you that Brownies do it better!"

His voice lowered to a more confidential tone.

"Listen, I know you fellows are in some trouble. It's not only that message from the young girl, would that I could remember it. I mean, we Brownies have eyes, you know. Any time you drop in on a group and they're in the middle of a pitched battle with the Netherhells, you can be sure they've got problems. Well, I tell you what I'm going to do for you. For the first time ever on this subcontinent, you folks are going to be the recipients of three wishes from—not Fairies—but Brownies!"

"Brownie wishes?" Snarks smiled a demon smile. "I take a size twelve."

The little fellow looked grieved. "Some day, when you've been saved by Brownie magic, you'll regret these remarks."

"Yes," Snarks replied. "But I have the feeling it will be a very small regret."

"Doom!" Headbasher once again flew through the air.

"Wuntvor?" the wizard called from where he stood in the distance. "May I see you for a moment?"

So this was the moment of truth. No longer would my master simply watch this drama unfold. There would be an accounting for my actions.

"Wuntvor." My master spoke softly as I approached. "I need to speak with you in earnest." He nodded toward a small rise nearby. "We can talk with more privacy on the far side of yonder hill."

Oh no. This was far worse than I first imagined. I had experienced wizardly rage before. Did Ebenezum wish to take me far enough away so the others would not hear him shouting?

The wizard turned. I followed him over the hill.

"All right!" the Brownie was shouting behind me. "I'll prove what I can do. I'll give you a little wish for free."

"I can think of a little wish," Snarks replied.

"Doom!" cried Hendrek.

"I'll behave! I'll behave!" Snarks shouted.

There was a crashing sound.

The noises behind us became muffled by distance.

"At last." Ebenezum paused and turned to me. "We can talk with some privacy."

The wizard cleared his throat. Quickly, I began to speak. Perhaps, if I explained what had happened with Norei before he asked, I could defuse the wizard's anger.

"Indeed." Ebenezum pulled at his beard. "Wuntvor, it is no wonder you cannot concentrate, with all that is going on on the far side of this hill. That, 'prentice, is the real reason I brought you here."

The wizard continued, his tone barely above a whisper. "I have noticed some problems with our current mode of travel. To be frank, our new companions seem to be rather more of a hindrance than a help."

I mentioned to my master the help the others had been in our battles with the Netherhells.

"True enough," the mage agreed. "But every battle has two sides, and that is true for all concerned. A few moments ago, Hendrek spoke about reaching Vushta with all haste. That is most assuredly true, and most assuredly a goal we are having great trouble attaining.

"There are certain things wrong with our party. If the Netherhells are looking for us, we definitely make an embarrassingly large and easy target. The only things moving with haste around here are the mouths of our companions."

The wizard sighed and scratched at the hair beneath his skullcap. " 'Tis true that all of our companions have their uses. Hendrek is quite good with that doomed club of his. Snarks knows things about the Netherhells that even I had not found out. And the Brownie . . ."

He hesitated for a moment, gazing back over the hill where our companions continued to argue. I think, at first, Ebenezum had wanted to dismiss the Brownie as just another of those peculiarities we had encountered in our travels. However, I could tell that the little fellow's remark about tax collectors had given the Brownie new respect in my master's eyes.

"No, we would be better off alone," he concluded. The wizard blew his nose briefly. "As you have no doubt noticed, I have another problem with our company. My malady reacts to all things magical—things such as Hendrek's club and the demon Snarks. It is troublesome to maintain allies when one is trying desperately to restrain a sneeze. The addition of the Brownie makes even that restraint impossible. For the sake of my nose, we must travel alone.

"Shoulder your pack, Wuntvor."

The wizard shrugged his robes back into place along his shoulders, and turned to walk down the path, away from the hill and our companions. " 'Tis better to move quickly to Vushta, and arrive there alive. Once we are among the company of magicians, we can do far more to help the likes of Snarks and Hendrek than we can in constant battle with the Netherhells."

I did as my master instructed, supporting myself with my stout oak staff as the wizard walked briskly before me.

"Master?" I asked hesitantly. "About Norei's warning? What if it has something to do with the two of us alone?"

The wizard pulled solemnly at his beard. "One way or another, we shall know soon enough. Come, Wuntvor. We need to gain some distance."

And so we walked again as we had through most of our journey, the wizard lost in sorcerous thought, while I brought along our belongings on my back—the arcane paraphernalia that had saved us a dozen times from death; a change of clothes; and lunch. I had to admit, there was a familiarity to this mode of travel that I found comforting. We set a sure pace with my master in the lead, and the forest seemed quieter with every step we took.

At length we reached a clearing. My master paused.

"Now, I think we have put sufficient distance between ourselves and our distractions. It's time, Wuntvor. We must speak with Norei."

I looked about the clearing. There didn't seem to be any birds at all in this part of the woods. But if my master wanted a communications spell, he would surely get one. It was so quiet in this spot, I could do nothing but succeed.

I thought of a grackle. A great brown bird, its

feathers shining in the sun. I whispered the proper mystic phrases, and launched myself from an imaginary branch, cawing at an imaginary sky. Norei! I was aloft, soaring above the clouds. Norei!

I saw my beloved's red hair, far below. I swooped down to be near her, plummetting through the air with tremendous speed. This time, I would learn her warning!

"Wuntvor?" Norei turned her face to the sky.

"Yes!" I cried, almost overcome with joy. "I—"

The wizard sneezed.

"Norei!" I called.

The earth shook at my feet. A fair quantity of dirt and pebbles showered both the wizard and myself.

No! Not now!

But there was no helping it. All thoughts of birds and Norei flew from my head. Insidiously foul demons! They attacked when we were at our weakest!

My master still sneezed uncontrollably. It was up to me, then, to handle the demons until the mage was sufficiently recovered to recite a spell. I waved my stout oak staff at the dust cloud that had risen with the explosion.

"There they are!" said a high, lilting, and all-too-familiar voice.

The dust lifted first from the ground, revealing a short fellow, about a foot-and-a-half high, dressed in a brown cloak and hood. To one side of him was someone in a long cloak; to the other, a pair of massive feet, legs and thighs.

The Brownie's legs were wobbling badly. He sat abruptly. "Excuse me, fellows. Just need to rest a moment."

"Doom!" a great voice boomed. "The Brownie has done what he promised!"

"Yeah, yeah," another, grating voice answered. "It isn't the gentlest way to travel, is it?" The dust was clearing now. I could discern the form of Snarks, trying to shake even more dirt from his robes.

"Now see what you have done!" Hendrek, spying my master, hastily replaced Headbasher in its protective sack. "Whatever fiendish plans of the Netherhells separated us from the wizard, the Brownie has reunited us, though it has taken all the strength in his tiny form!" He glowered at Snarks. The demon retreated behind his voluminous robes.

"Gzzphttx!" Snarks replied.

"Doom," Hendrek murmured softly. He turned to the wizard and myself. "Thank the gods we have found you. Apparently, the plans of the Netherhells are even more nefarious than we imagined. They will separate us, and cut us down brutally, one by one!"

My master stroked his long, white beard. "Indeed," he remarked. "We must be continually more vigilant."

Hendrek pointed the sack containing Headbasher at the little fellow sitting in the dirt. "Thank the gods we have this noble Brownie as our companion."

"Oh no!" the Brownie cried and leapt to his feet. "That wasn't big enough to be a wish! You folks had asked for a demonstration or two. I just wanted to show you the full extent of Brownie Power! The three wishes come next!"

I looked to my master. This quiet corner of the forest had suddenly become as noisy as every place else. We had lost our solitude, and our chance to learn Norei's warning. Yet my master stood in the midst of it all, stroking his beard, the picture of calm. All in all, he seemed to be taking it very well.

" 'Tis true," my master remarked when there was finally a pause in the conversation. He cleared his sorcerous throat. "We are in a perilous situation, the true extent of which is not yet known. For the good of us all, we may have to make some special arrangements."

"Doom," Hendrek remarked. "What do you mean, great wizard?"

"Oh, only that we should spread out a bit so that we do not form such an obvious target for the plots of the Netherhells." The wizard sniffed. "But that is only the second most important thing we must remember."

The large warrior looked suspiciously around the clearing. "And the first?"

"That, no matter what, we keep walking." The wizard turned and marched out of the clearing. "If there are no objections?"

"Snrrzbffl!" Snarks lifted his robes and pointed to what appeared to be a new pair of shoes upon his demon feet.

"Oh, did I make the shoes a little bit too tight?" The Brownie shook his head in sympathy.

"Gffttbbll!"

"No, no, the one thing Brownies really know about are shoes. You said that yourself." The Brownie ran to follow the marching wizard.

"To Vushta!" Hendrek cried, falling in close behind the Brownie's tiny feet.

I shouldered my pack and gripped my stout oak staff. Grumbling deep within his hood, Snarks took up the rear. We were marching at last, on to our goal. Nothing would stop us now.

Then, at the edge of the forest, we saw the unicorn.

FOUR

There is talk in some learned circles in our major cities about whether or not satyrs, centaurs, griffins and certain other fantastic beasts really exist, or are only the product of the popular imagination. As a wizard, I, of course, tend to side with the satyrs, centaurs and griffins, especially when these beasts begin to doubt the existence of any learned circles in our major cities.

—*THE TEACHINGS OF EBENEZUM,*
VOLUME XXXVI

The unicorn ran in our direction.

I forgot to walk. All I could do was stare.

"Doo—oof!" Hendrek exclaimed loudly as he walked into my overloaded pack. He began a loud and complicated curse.

I placed a hand upon his shoulder to quiet him, and pointed at the approaching beast. Hendrek's complaints stopped midsentence as his mouth opened, unable to form further words. All of his attention, and mine as well, was drawn to the newcomer.

How do I describe that creature? Its golden hooves would stamp upon any words I might use, grinding them to inconsequential dust. Still, what can humans do but try?

Imagine a horse, if you will, a horse of pure white, its color that of the snow as it falls fresh from the clouds, before it is sullied by the common air. It is a swift horse, in its prime, lean but powerful. Its muscles ripple beneath its coat as it leaps through the stillness, and, when its hooves touch ground, the earth shakes with its passing.

Ah, but this creature is more than a mere horse, for atop its white head, before its wildly cascading mane, is a golden horn as long as my arm. The horn is not quite straight, and yet not truly curved, as if neither the line nor the circle were special enough to give it form. And it rises above the creature's head as if it were reaching for the sun.

I spoke of the sun. It had, in fact, appeared before us. We had come to a clearing. The close trees that we had toiled through for the past few days spread apart to reveal a good-sized meadow filled with flowers and long, deep green grass. Patches of light shone upon this field through broken clouds, as if the sun had sewn a quilted pattern upon the earth.

How I had complained about the dank and dreary forest we had labored through for so long! How dearly I had longed to see true sunlight! But now, I only noticed the sun because it reflected off the back of the approaching beast. And the white of the unicorn's coat seemed as bright as the sun itself.

Somehow, it was only proper. If we were to see the sun for the first time after so many days, it should be at a wonderful moment such as this. How else could we do honor to such a regal beast?

The unicorn reared up before us. It was even more astonishing to look at close at hand, the very heart of magic brought to life. It stood but a dozen paces away, magnificent, the essence of peace and bearing, contentment and beauty. Except that there was something about the way the creature blinked its large and soulful eyes.

"How could they!" the splendid creature exclaimed.

Ebenezum blew his nose. He moved a few steps to the left, careful, I was sure, to remain upwind of the magnificent beast.

"Indeed," the wizard remarked quietly. "How could they what?"

The unicorn eyed us warily, then glanced rapidly back over its grandly beautiful shoulder. "Well, I barely know where to begin. There I was, minding my unicorn business, when they attacked me!"

The perfect beast snorted in dismay.

"Pray continue." The wizard pulled reflectively upon his long beard. "You were attacked? By demons?"

"No, no!" the unicorn cried. "Far worse than that! Mere demons I would have gored and tossed aside! But to be attacked by such as these!" A tremor passed through the beast's stately frame.

"What they did! I can barely speak about it even now. They tied my golden hooves, these hooves meant to run free over the green and verdant sward! They covered my golden horn, the center of my beauty and my defense against injustice! They bound it round with common pillows, saying, 'We don't want any accidental stabbings, ha ha.' Pillows about my magnificent golden horn! And, and—" The unicorn paused, swallowing deep within its splendid throat. Its voice lowered to a whisper. "And they mussed my stately, flowing mane!"

"Indeed?" my master replied.

"My flowing mane!" The unicorn nodded its head vehemently. "Can you imagine, handled roughly like that? They have no respect for my species at all. And not a virgin among them, either! Well, you know, that's not at all surprising in this part of the forest, but still . . ."

The unicorn snorted mightily. It appeared too overwhelmed to go on.

A large shadow passed over our heads.

The unicorn screamed.

" 'Tis them!" the stately beast cried. "They have found me!" The unicorn glanced nervously aloft. "You weren't listening, were you? I'm distraught! I didn't know what I was saying! I didn't mean what I said about virgins! Honestly!"

The shadow was gone.

"Indeed." My master spoke in his most reassuring tone, honed to a fine art through years of use placating rich clients and distracting tax collectors. "Whoever they were, they seem to be gone now. If you are in distress, perhaps we can help you. Tell me, is there any money involved?"

"What use have magical creatures for money?" The unicorn tossed its perfectly formed head to and fro in despair. "How could I ever expect mere humans to understand?"

"Okay. It's time for an expert." The Brownie stepped forward. "Enchanted creature to enchanted creature, we will learn the truth. And I won't even count it as a wish. That's Brownie Power for you!"

"No, no, I've said far too much already!" The unicorn shied away from its small interrogator.

The Brownie stepped even closer, undaunted by the splendid beast's greater size. "All right!" the small fellow said. "Let's get to the heart of the matter.

What's all this guff about virgins?''

"What?" The unicorn shook its head. "Why, it's just something unicorns do. It's expected of us, you know, like Brownies making shoes.''

"And we're going to change all that!" the Brownie cried. "Brownies do it better!" The little person cleared his throat. "Pardon. Just hit a sore spot there.'' He shot an accusatory look back at Snarks, still hidden deep within voluminous robes. "I've always been interested in this. Do unicorns really seek out virgins?"

"Actually, no,'' the snow-white beast replied. "I've always thought the unicorn's essential task was to frolic through distant fields while looking ethereally beautiful. Virgins are really a sideline. But we know one when we see one. There's one here, in fact.''

All around me there was an intake of breath.

"Yes. Somebody's a virgin. I can always tell, you know. It's something we unicorns are very good at.'' The beast tossed its head jauntily. "Of course, we unicorns are good at *so* many things!''

"Wait a second,'' I interjected, somewhat unsettled by this line of conversation. "Don't virgins have to be female?"

"A popular misconception. No, a virgin is a virgin, male or female, and I scent one nearby.'' The unicorn looked from Hendrek to me and back again.

"Doom,'' the large warrior intoned.

The creature's scrutiny was very discomforting. Just what was this overmuscled animal implying? Snarks made a low, snickering noise deep within his hood.

"Well.'' The wizard once again stepped forward, his robes discreetly covering his nose. "I'm sure this is all very interesting, but could you tell us exactly who you are running from?"

"Running?" The unicorn stamped its golden hooves

upon the earth. "Unicorns run from no one! Well,
that's not quite true. Let's just say the intelligent
unicorn knows who to avoid." The beast glanced nervously overhead.

The wizard blew his nose. "And who, indeed, might
that be?"

The unicorn lowered its gaze from the sky. "I have
said far too much already." It turned its head slightly to
look at all of us, then pointed briefly with its horn.
"Just don't go that way."

The beast's horn pointed toward Vushta.

"I have said all that I can. May you be blessed with a
unicorn's luck." The mighty beast reared up, then
galloped into the dark forest from which we had come.

"A unicorn's blessing!" Snarks had removed his
hood. "If what that fancy horse has been through is
unicorn luck, it should be as much use to us as three
Brownie wishes!"

The demon rapidly replaced his hood as the Brownie
approached.

"Doom," Hendrek intoned. "Dare we go farther, to
face whatever dread thing yon beast has escaped?"

"We must," the wizard insisted. "Put your club
away, would you? That's a good fellow. In this instance, I believe friend Snarks has made a valid point.
Information, the wise man knows, is only as good as its
source. A source whose main concern is how much its
mane has been mussed is hardly any source at all."

"Whatever happens," a small voice piped, "you have
a Brownie at your side!"

"Indeed. And I am sure we will be properly grateful
when the time comes."

"But what of Norei's warning?" I asked. "Could the
unicorn have seen something?"

"Would that I knew, Wuntvor." The wizard stared

up at a sky filled with skittering clouds, hoping, perhaps, to see what had frightened the unicorn so. "If this were a perfect world, I might take some time and study this matter, using the full body of my learning and experience to reach a learned, truly wizardly decision. Unfortunately, this world appears to be getting less perfect every day. Things are happening much too fast to depend upon wizardly conjecture."

My master tugged his robes into more aesthetically pleasing lines. "We must rely, therefore, entirely on wizardly intuition! Wuntvor, shoulder your pack! On to Vushta!"

So saying, Ebenezum led us across the clearing to another stretch of nearly impenetrable forest. I paused for an instant, savoring a last glimpse of golden sunlight before we were once again surrounded by great, dark trees.

Far behind us, I heard the unicorn scream.

"I have an idea what you can use for your first wish."

I jumped at the sound of the Brownie's voice.

"Sorry!" the small voice piped. "I do tend to be enthusiastic. Part of my overall Positive Brownie Image, you know."

I looked back in the direction of the unicorn's cry, but the trees blocked my view.

"Can you wish us out of here?" I asked.

"Sorry. We just tried that, bringing your friends here." The Brownie frowned and shook his head. "Puts too much strain on the magic muscles."

The Brownie paused. I realized belatedly that he was expecting me to keep up my end of the conversation. I was too busy listening for the unicorn, or whatever the unicorn had seen.

"What wish did you have in mind?" I asked at last.

"That's more like it!" the Brownie replied. "You

have to get in the spirit of this three wishes thing, you know. My job is to make the wishes happen! I don't have time to think them up as well!"

I nodded. The Brownie certainly had a point. Somehow, though, things had been too busy lately for me to think about wishing for anything.

"I know, I know," the Brownie went on. "My performance up to now has not been exemplary. That's why I feel I have to push the wishes bit a little. Remember the Brownie Creed: It's not magic—it's Brownie Power!"

The Brownie continued in a whisper. "I have been observing your master. A sad case, a great wizard like that, unable to perform magic because of a malady of the nose. See? We Brownies notice things like that! And this Brownie knows a cure!"

I turned to look at the small fellow. A cure? Hope rose within me like the sun lighting a summer dawn. If Ebenezum could regain his powers, we would reach Vushta in no time at all!

"I know it will work." The small one's voice became softer still. "It has to do with shoes."

My hope plummeted like a winter storm. This was the Brownie who had trouble remembering people's names, let alone the messages they had given him. Maybe Snarks was right about him after all.

The little fellow glanced somewhat apprehensively at the demon, who was walking now at Hendrek's side. It was almost as if the Brownie had read my mind.

"Some may laugh at me," he continued in a whisper, "but always start with what you know best. That's what His Brownieship says."

His Brownieship? I decided not to ask.

"Anyways, I can make a shoe big enough to protect your master from magical influences." The Brownie paused and tapped his tiny foot. "I can see that you're skeptical. Well, just wait 'til you see it! Hands-on experience, that's what we need here. I just have to have a little while to get my notes together, and, next time we have a crisis, one Brownie shoe special will do the trick!"

My master began to sneeze.

"Doom!" Hendrek bellowed, looking in the trees overhead.

"It's time for the shoe!" I cried to the Brownie, but my voice was drowned out by the beating of gigantic wings.

FIVE

A wizard must do his best not to judge any person or thing on their first appearance. Many a human or other intelligent creature will have hidden depths to their personalities which you will only discover as you get to know them and work with them; and hidden cash reserves, which you can bill them for regularly as this aforementioned knowledge process takes place.

—*THE TEACHINGS OF EBENEZUM,*
VOLUME LVI

I was pushed to the ground. Something grabbed me. Something as hard as rock. I was lifted into the air as I might lift an insect from a leaf.

I looked down at the rapidly receding earth to see Snarks, Hendrek and the Brownie staring up in horror. Where was my master?

There was a sneeze close by my left ear. I managed to turn my head against the wind, and saw my master, clasped within a giant yellow claw. I looked down at the hard yellow ridges that contained me, and realized that I was held by a claw as well.

The thing had me clutched facing down. I found it impossible to crane my head any farther to discern the true nature of our captor. Perhaps, considering the size of the claws, ignorance was bliss. I could only look at the rapidly moving ground far below and wish that I had not eaten such a heavy lunch.

We were moving at fantastic speed. I felt as if the wind might tear the clothes from my already-chilled body. It roared in my ears and made tears stream down my face. I cried out against the wind, full of fear and anger. What could be worse than this?

And then the thing's claw began to open.

I clutched for a hold on the horny yellow flesh. Rather we should be carried aloft and windblown forever than be dashed among the trees far below! But the trees were getting closer. In my panic, I had not noticed how far the thing had descended.

Suddenly, we were above a clearing filled with milling people. No, no, they weren't people. They were something else entirely.

That's when the claw let me go.

As I picked myself up, my first thoughts were for my master. But there he was beside me, his deep blue wizard's robes in disarray. His fine magician's cap was gone, but otherwise he seemed to have survived intact. He was, of course, sneezing profusely.

Something roared mightily nearby. Instinctively, I reached for my stout oak staff. It was nowhere around me. I realized with a chill that both my staff and pack were gone!

It would have to be my fists, then. I stared at the ground for an instant, calming myself, steeling my resolve to battle until my last ounce of strength was gone, for Ebenezum, and Vushta!

I looked up into the face of the strangest creature I had ever seen.

"Do you have any gold?" the face rumbled. It was the face of a very large eagle. The body of the creature, however, was not birdlike at all, but was rather that of a lion. Was this what I had heard roar before? It had not been a very friendly sound. Then, of course, there were the creature's great wings, not to mention the tail, which looked like the latter half of one of the longest snakes I had ever seen. All in all, I was understandably taken aback.

The creature growled, obviously upset that I had not answered him.

"I repeat," it said, "do you have any gold?"

What could I say? I had no idea whether we had any gold or not. Ebenezum always handled all our money matters. But being in the presence of what was obviously an enchanted beast, my master's sneezing fit now consumed him entirely.

The beast's serpent tail began to twitch in an agitated manner. The creature opened its beak and emitted a sound far worse than words. It began as the cry of an eagle and ended as the roar of a lion, embodying the harsher characteristics of both calls. All in all, it was quite unpleasant.

"Oh, Pop, come off it!" Another magical beast, this one with the head and wings of an eagle and the body of a horse, galloped between us. "Can't you see you're scaring the pants off this guy?"

"There are certain customs that must be observed," the father said stiffly. "Griffins always look for gold."

"But we're here to change all that, remember?"

"Ah, yes." The Griffin made a strangled noise deep in his throat. "We'll talk about it later, when we're alone. He's a bright lad," it said to no one in particular. "A little headstrong, but bright."

"But Pop! You have to tell them!"

The Griffin turned and roared at its son.

"I don't have to do anything!"

"But Pop! Why else would we bring them here?"

"Ah, yes." The Griffin paused again. "That is true." The beast turned to me. "You have been abducted for a reason."

The eagle/horse walked over to my still-sneezing master.

"You know, Pop, this guy looks like he's in a lot of trouble."

"Do you have to keep interrupting me!" The Griffin raked its claws through the tall grass before him. The grass became considerably shorter. "Youngsters! Nothing's good enough for them anymore! Well, let me tell you something, son. I've had more than enough of your interference!"

"I was just trying to help!" The youngster stamped its left forehoof. "It takes you forever to do anything!"

"No respect!" The Griffin growled deeply. "When I was your age, nobody wore his feathers that long! You're a disgrace to the mythical community!"

Ebenezum covered himself with his robes. The sneezing continued unabated.

"We've really got to do something with this guy." The youngster nudged Ebenezum gently with its beak. "It doesn't do any good to talk to them if they're dead."

"Oh, very well." The Griffin turned back to me. "Are you sure you don't have any gold?" It nodded its beak at a couple of nearby creatures. "Shake them up and down and see if they clink."

The younger creature was right. Ebenezum was in sad shape. I didn't think a good shaking would improve his health. Hurriedly, I remarked that, even if we had had any gold, we would have lost it during our ride here.

The Griffin sighed. "True enough. That's one problem with the Rok. He's fast enough, but he's not very bright." The beast stared at me with an eagle eye. "He's the exception, of course. Most of us are quite talented."

"Maybe we should let them rest awhile," the youngster suggested gently. "There's that old shack over—"

"Be quiet and let your elders think! Youngsters!" The Griffin paused, then raised a wing in triumph. "Of course! There's that old shack over there! It's out of the wind. The sneezing human can get warm and dry. After a few hours, he'll be ready to talk!"

"You mean *listen*, don't you, Pop?"

The Griffin caught itself midroar. "Ah, yes. My son is right. We'll have our meeting tomorrow then, at dawn." It shook its head sadly. "Why is there never any gold? It's hard on an old Griffin, let me tell you."

A couple of creatures with the bodies of horses and the chests, heads and faces of men helped hoist the helplessly sneezing wizard onto the back of the eagle/horse. Apparently, even though the Griffin was still muttering about the lack of gold and his place in society, we weren't supposed to pay any attention to him anymore. Certainly nobody else was.

"Centaurs," the youngster said to my confused expression. He took off at a good trot. I had to run to keep up.

"Excuse me," I ventured, trying to make sense out of this whole thing. "Is that what you are? A Centaur?" Somehow, I had the feeling that this creature's head was

all wrong for that classification. I added lamely:
"You're not a Griffin, are you?"

The youngster laughed heartily. "Boy, you don't
have your mythology down at all, do you? I'm a Hippogriff. Actually, I'm *the* Hippogriff, as far as I
know."

Was that something my master should have taught
me? Perhaps every apprentice worth his name
automatically knew what a Hippogriff was. On occasion, when we found ourselves in difficult situations
such as these, I did wish I had made it just a little further
with my wizardly apprenticeship.

"You're the only Hippogriff, then?" I replied, doing
my best to seem polite. Though it is difficult to feign interest when your master may be sneezing his life away.
"What," I added after a moment, "is there not much
call for the job?"

The Hippogriff looked at me far more soberly. "On
the contrary. Since I'm the first, writing the job descrip-
tion is up to me." It looked down proudly at its
hooves. "I am unique, the product of true interspecies
romance."

"Interspecies romance?" I asked. I realized as soon
as the words were out of my mouth that this matter
might be too delicate for common conversation.

"Of course." The Hippogriff fluffed its wings out
proudly. Well, the creature didn't seem to mind, then.
Still, I would have felt on much firmer ground in this
situation if I could have told just when an eagle was
smiling. "You've met my father. My mother was a
horse. All in all, I would say a fine combination."

"You mean," I asked, temporarily taken aback by
the very thought, "that you can have—uh—romantic
interludes with any animal that interests you?"

"Certainly. Birds and fish, too!"

The whole idea left me momentarily speechless. I was all too familiar with the problems presented by romance with human females. Romance with nearly anything that moved was a truly overwhelming concept. A wizard's apprentice needs to be ready for all occurrences. Still, having a love affair with a trout was virtually beyond my comprehension.

"You seem a bit taken aback," the Hippogriff remarked. "Trust me, it's a truly liberating experience." The creature's voice lowered to a more confidential tone. "I tell you, right now there's this little ocelot I have my eye on. Woo Woo!" The Hippogriff smacked its beak.

"Ah! Here we are!" The Hippogriff sat, depositing the bundle of still-sneezing wizard at the front door of what could in charity be called a dilapidated shack. The boards of what once were sturdy walls sagged inward on all sides, as if the shack was trying hard to return to its earlier state of being as a pile of lumber. There was something that might once have been a window on one side of the structure, plus a couple of even more ragged holes elsewhere that appeared to have occurred sometime after the shack was built.

"Our best accommodations," the Hippogriff remarked. "This should give your friend here a chance to rest. It's away from the hustle and bustle of the rest of the beasts. Your only neighbor is the unicorn we've got penned up just beyond those trees. What a bore, that unicorn, always going on about virgins. Who knows anything about virgins?"

I agreed hastily.

"Oh, by the way," the Hippogriff added, "please don't think of escaping. There's a lot of beasts among us who are very good at finding humans, and some aren't as gentle in their transportation as our friend the

Rok. Have a nice night." The Hippogriff turned and galloped away.

My master took a deep breath and, for a change, did not sneeze. He groaned instead. I looked at the clouds gathering in the late afternoon sky. I decided I should get him inside what little shelter the shack would provide.

A piece of frayed rope was tied to the door. I pulled, praying the crumbling hemp would hold long enough for the door to swing out. There was a rending noise. I tossed the door, now free of its hinges, aside and carried my master into the shack's interior. The place had a dirt floor. I placed my master in the very center of the small room, as far away from the crazily leaning walls as possible.

Ebenezum groaned again, then raised himself to his elbows and blew his nose.

" 'Tis a nightmare, Wuntvor," was all he could manage before he had to catch his breath.

I asked my master to rest. There must be a stream nearby. I would pop out for a minute and bring us back some water.

I stepped to the door, and startled two winged creatures. They flew up with cawing screams that ran down my spine like ice. Their appearance had unsettled me almost as much as I had frightened them. The things had the bodies of vultures, but the heads of beautiful women.

I almost stumbled over the buckets they had left behind. One was filled with water, the other with something hot and steamy that looked like stew. Well, I reflected, at least our captors were taking care of us. If what I had seen so far was indicative of the rest of them, I hoped they would continue to take care of us from the greatest distance possible.

I grabbed a bucket in each hand and took them inside to my master.

Ebenezum had sat up in my absence and, besides the fact that he had lost his cap, looked reasonably well composed.

"Indeed," he murmured as I placed the two buckets before him. He pulled two wooden spoons from the stew and handed one to me. "All the comforts of home."

The wind gusted outside. The shack creaked horribly.

"As temporary as our home may be," Ebenezum added as he spooned a mouthful of stew.

The food was bland but palatable, with many vegetables and some sort of thankfully unidentifiable meat. As my stomach filled, I considered that it had probably been prepared to satisfy the needs of the greatest variety of creatures possible. Satiated at last, I inquired how my master felt.

"Remarkably well, all things taken into account," Ebenezum replied when he was done licking his spoon. "One feels much better when one can breathe. The first bout of sneezing tends to clear the nasal passages." He rubbed his nose absently. " 'Tis a little sore, but, with a good night's sleep, I will survive."

The wizard rubbed his stomach. "Indeed," he said after a moment's pause. "We seem to have but one or two small problems here. First, there is far too much magic about here for my malady. I do not think these creatures necessarily mean to do us harm, for they took note of my sneezing, and gave us accommodations so that I might recover." He glanced absently at the swaying walls. "Then again, perhaps they put us here to be rid of us altogether. I don't think this shack would survive a summer shower."

The wizard pulled his gaze away from the creaking

wood and turned back to me. "Second, they have separated us from the rest of our party, although that may, in a way, be more blessing than curse. Still, along with our companions we have lost both personal belongings and some very important magical gear. With the limits of my sorcery of late, I had come to depend more and more on my arcane paraphernalia. I shall miss it."

My master paused again. His fingers, which had been playing absently with his beard, tightened into a fist.

"Third, and by far the most serious, we are no longer able to travel to Vushta. The world seems to be unravelling faster than any of us can hold it together. Tonight I must sleep. Tomorrow, we will listen to what these beasts have to say, but we cannot stay here longer. If they do not let us leave freely, we will escape in the night."

I shivered involuntarily.

My master nodded. "And we will have to deal with whatever terrible things they send after us. We must, to defeat the Netherhells!"

So we sat for a minute, listening to the shack complain at an occasional gust of wind. I realized that, much to my surprise, it was perfectly quiet. For the first time in half a day, I thought of my own true love.

"I must talk with Norei," I said. "I think I can do it now."

"An excellent plan, Wuntvor! While it is hard to imagine us in more difficulty than we are at present. Still, my age and wisdom tell me that it can get far worse. At this juncture, any assistance from any source would be most welcome." My master rubbed his nose again. "Except, may I suggest that when you perform the necessary magic, you do it outside our shelter?"

It was little enough to ask. I stepped through the doorway, and looked about in the twilight for the piece of rotting wood I had discarded before. I propped it as best I could against the doorway, shutting my master away as much as possible from the outside world and the magic that I was about to perform.

The wind had died, as it often does at evening, and the world seemed strangely serene. Clouds still covered a good part of the sky, but where they broke I could see the stars. It was nice to be outside, on my own, in the quiet dark. But I should not let a temporary feeling of well-being distract me from my task. Every moment I dallied was another moment the Netherhells could further their plans. I would contact Norei, and gain what knowledge and help that I could.

After a moment's thought, I decided to move a bit farther from the shack in which my master slept. The greater the distance, I thought, the kinder it would be to his nose. I would not go too far; the clouds above made the night very dark. Still, there was a copse of trees nearby. If I were to perform my magic just beyond that natural barrier, I would be able to find my way back handily when the task was done. I walked slowly across the field, careful of sinkholes and hidden roots. Already, my mind was filled with thoughts of flying grackles. I would make my master proud of me!

I passed through the trees even more carefully, lest I trip over some bush or sapling in the blackness. Soon, though, I had won my way through to the other side, where I came to a wooden fence. It was a sturdy piece of construction, and held my weight well when I leaned against it. I decided I would prop my back against it as I said my spell.

I said the magic words and thought of a grackle.

Once again, my thoughts took flight, this time through the night sky above the clouds. It was a new world up here, awash with countless points of pale light which made the clouds below into rolling hills, like the world must have looked before the coming of man and beast. As I flew, I felt like I was a small star myself, brother to all the other stars in the heavens.

Some sense given me by the spell guided me on my way. I was near. I spread my wings and dived through the clouds, confident I would see my true love anon.

I couldn't see a thing. The clouds had grown together as I flew, blotting out the stars. How could I find my true love's flaming red hair when there was no way in the blackness to tell red from green or purple? I cried out my despair; the rough caw of a grackle.

"Wuntvor!" The voice was far away. I did not so much hear it as feel it in my mind. But I knew the voice was Norei's.

"Beloved!" I cried in return, being careful to keep the grackle's image firm in my mind. This apprentice was not going to make the same mistake twice! "Norei! Where are you?"

"Follow my voice!" she cried, and I obeyed gladly. "I am beneath the trees!" I swooped lower, skimming the treetops. The forest went on forever!

"Here!" she called. "I can sense you near!"

I plunged through the leaves. Where was I? There was rustling all around me. I was so close now! I couldn't get lost in the upper branches! I flapped my wings, and broke through to clear air beneath the trees. And there, before me, stood Norei!

She smiled up at me. Her perfect lips opened and she called, "Well done, Wuntvor!"

It was enough to make all my feathers stand on end. I cawed with happiness! Oh, if only my magic beak would turn to lips, I would kiss that perfect mouth 'til all the breath had left my mortal form!

"Wuntvor, please!" Norei laughed, the sound of tiny

bells ushering in springtime. "Wuntvor, stop! Your feathers tickle!"

I pulled up short, and almost lost the grackle in my mind. My magical form had far more substance than I had imagined. I started to stammer out an apology.

"There's no time for that now!" Norei replied. "We must talk while the spell holds us together!"

Yes, yes, talk! Norei, my beloved! How long had I wished to see your sweet face—

"Wuntvor!" My beloved's voice had developed a stern edge. "You are sweet, but sometimes—" She sighed. "Your spell is far too delicate. It's liable to be broken at any moment! We must talk about the Nether-hells!"

Yes, yes, of course, she was right. I was here to get her message, the important warning the Brownie had told us about!

"Wuntvor, the Netherhells have embarked on the most diabolical plan in the history of the world!"

Yes, yes, my beloved! Ebenezum discerned this as well! The Netherhells wish to take the surface world and make it their own! That's why we must rush to Vushta and rally our strength!

Norei paused. Was that the limit of her message? I felt a brief disappointment. Had I anticipated this moment for so long, only to have Norei tell me something I already knew?

"I see," she said at last. "Then do you know about the Forxnagel?"

Not the Forxnagel! The shock was so great, I once again nearly lost my grackle form. The Forxnagel was the overspell. He who successfully completed it would control all magic everywhere. We had once defeated an inept magician who had attempted this all-powerful magic. But the denizens of the Netherhells were far from inept! This was much worse than I imagined!

"What, you knew that, too?" Norei had taken my shocked silence for silent indifference. Vexation was entering her voice. "Maybe I shouldn't have even spoken to the Brownie! Well, how about this, then? It's the most important part. Do you know about the fate the Netherhells have particularly planned for the Wizard?"

"What?" I cawed in alarm.

"Well, good. I'm glad I didn't call you for no reason whatever. It's a shame to waste magic." Norei smiled ever so slightly before her earnest expression returned.

"They're very specific about it. Ebenezum has quite an enemy in the Netherhells, a powerful demon named Guxx Unfufadoo."

A chill went down my feathered spine. The warning had to do with Guxx? The situation was becoming more desperate with every passing moment.

"Guxx has plans for your master," Norei continued. "Hideously demonic plans. Listen carefully, if you wish to save his life—"

"Yes, my belov—," I began. I felt a pain in my chest. No, not the chest of the magic grackle, but my human chest, so many miles away from Norei.

I was being stabbed!

SIX

There comes a time when every wizard should retire, and pass the mantle of responsibility on to younger shoulders. It behooves us, then, to teach our successors well, so that the new wizard may do honor to our names, attract the very best of clients, and be well enough paid to support our retirement home in Vushta.

—*THE TEACHINGS OF EBENEZUM,*
VOLUME LXXI

It was the unicorn. It stood across the fence from me, its golden horn pressing into my chest.

"Oh good," the magnificent beast said. "You're awake. You seemed to be having the strangest dream. Tell me. Do you often caw in your sleep?"

I stepped back from the horn. This is what had startled me away from my beloved, just as I was about to receive her true message!

"Why?" I asked, struggling to form words, my head still half-full of grackle. "What do you want?"

59

The beast sighed. "Unicorns, beautiful though we are, get lonely, too."

"You woke me up because you were lonely?" I was incredulous.

"Yes." The unicorn fluttered its dark, soulful eyes. "That, and I was looking for a virgin lap somewhere, to lay my head."

"Get away from me!" I cried. This was too much!

"Come on now," the unicorn pleaded. "Here I am, trapped by a bunch of uncouth beasts, unable to roam the verdant fields as is my right. Do you know how tedious it can get, all by yourself with no one to admire you?"

I wanted to scream. I had lost Norei because some creature wanted me to admire it? My beloved hadn't told me her message! I had to go back. I did my best to think of a grackle.

It was no use. I was too upset. Anger killed my concentration. How could things get any worse?

It started to rain.

The shack survived the summer shower. It did so by leaking in every conceivable location. I perceived, at last, why the shack was still standing. Water could not damage the old structure, since the old structure simply let the rain pass on through, straight down upon us.

In short, we did not have the most restful of nights.

Something pounded on our door around dawn.

"Wake up! Rise and shine! We're all waiting for you!"

We? Waiting for what? I realized that I had talked to the Hippogriff for quite some time yesterday without learning anything of substance. Well, there was always interspecies romance, but I didn't feel that was appropriate to our present situation. At least, I hoped it wasn't.

The door fell in. It hit the muddy earth with a sickening plop.

Ebenezum rolled over and groaned. The Hippogriff stuck its eagle head inside.

"My, my," the creature said. "All right, we'll give you a few minutes to pull yourselves together. You're guests of honor, you know."

Ebenezum sat up and sneezed.

"I'll wait a respectful distance away," the Hippogriff said, withdrawing its head. "I know how you humans value your privacy."

"Wuntvor," Ebenezum said hoarsely after the Hippogriff had gone. "I cannot go out there."

I looked to my master. This trip had been more than hard on him. He had rallied above his difficulties time and time again, saying spells to remove us from danger even though he might sneeze for hours thereafter. But our adventures had taken a toll upon the wizard. A half-dozen times on our journey thus far, my master's ills had overwhelmed his sorcerous spirit, and his aura of wizardliness would leave him for an hour or two, leaving only an old man behind.

Now, I could see that fatigue about his eyes once again. The day before had been far too taxing on his constitution. He needed rest desperately. He needed to be kept far away from anything that would cause a nasal reaction.

Now the Hippogriff was going to take us to a meeting of monsters. And, as far as my master's malady went, the assemblage out there was ragweed season. If my master took that trip out there today, I feared it would be the last trip he would ever take.

"I will handle it myself," I proclaimed. Before my master could protest, I walked out to meet the Hippogriff in the yard.

"Where's the other one?" the beast inquired.

"I'm the one who makes decisions," I lied. "The other one is old, and you saw that he was sick. If we need him, we can talk to him later."

The Hippogriff considered my words. "But, isn't he the wizard? I mean, I'm not really up on human attire, but those were wizard's robes he was wearing, weren't they?"

The Hippogriff had a point. I had to think fast. How could I convince the beasts that Ebenezum was unimportant, so that they would let the wizard rest and regain his strength?

"Well, the old fellow was a wizard, once. Quite a good one, too. He still can conjure a trick or two, on his better days. We let him keep the robes. It's an honorary sort of thing. But you notice he doesn't have a hat. Only full-fledged wizards can have hats."

"You, then, are a full-fledged wizard?" the beast asked.

I nodded solemnly.

"So where's your hat?"

My hand involuntarily brushed my hair. "Well, yes, indeed. A bit embarrassing, that. I'm afraid I lost it when the Rok brought us here."

The Hippogriff shrugged its equine shoulders.

"All right, I guess. It's a bit of a problem with the Rok, always losing things. Even passengers, sometimes—" The Hippogriff nodded solemnly, as if carefully reviewing the situation. "You'll just have to explain it to Pop. I'll warn you, though, should you in any way try to play him false. Griffins have a very low tolerance for lies."

I waved away the Hippogriff's warning with the back of my hand, as if to say, "What need has a wizard to fear a Griffin's anger?" I did my best to walk by the Hippogriff's side without my knees buckling beneath me from fright.

My master must recover. Otherwise, we would never see Vushta, and the world would be lost to demons.

I told myself that over and over again as we approached the crowd of monsters.

"You know, of course," the Hippogriff remarked, "we observed your party for some time before we requested your presence before our assembly."

"Indeed?" I replied. Had they observed us long enough to realize I was nothing more than an apprentice?

"Yes, our organization wants to be careful in how we are presented to the human world. We wanted the best possible spokespeople to carry our story beyond the Enchanted Forest."

"Indeed!" I said, as firmly as possible. Perhaps I shouldn't be worried after all. We must have made a pretty good impression. My legs seemed firmer beneath me now, my feet striding boldly along the path. If they thought that much of me, I must walk like a wizard.

"Of course, finding any spokespeople at all was a bit of a problem in the Enchanted Forest. For some reason, this is the sort of place people tend to avoid. Probably has something to do with a large number of our membership having a taste for human flesh."

My knees threatened to go altogether. I cleared my throat. "Indeed," I managed after a moment.

"Don't worry, though. The membership has sworn off eating humans until the end of this campaign. Well, at least most of them have, and I'm sure we can crush any dissidents before they have time to nibble more than a toe or two. So really, you have nothing to worry about. You just keep your part of the bargain, and you'll be perfectly safe."

I nodded my head, trying to look far more sure of myself than I felt. What bargain, where? Safe from what? My voice had died in my throat. I couldn't even manage another "indeed."

"So there we were," the Hippogriff continued, "looking for spokespeople, when who should come crashing through the forest but you five. Now the Rok can only carry two at a time, so we had to figure out who it was best to invite. Luckily, it didn't take long to make that decision. The older wizard and you seemed to be the only ones actually doing anything."

I thought on that for a moment. "Well, the others are very good talkers."

"You got it!" The Hippogriff nodded to the assembled masses before us. "Wait a moment, and you'll see that we, too, are great masters of rhetoric."

The Hippogriff led me through the assembled creatures and monstrosities to a raised platform in their midst. I was aware of a thousand eyes upon me, the eyes of birds and beasts and men, although the bodies that went with those eyes were often of a different species altogether. I glanced about briefly as we moved through the assemblage. I—who had seen a thousand demons, each one different from the last, and who had witnessed other wonders uncountable in my travels toward Vushta—I saw any number of creatures I'd never seen before. I got a sense of every sort of fur and feather, small eyes hidden behind shaggy manes, large eyes on the ends of stalks, and, of course, large teeth and even larger teeth, claws and pincers and long, barbed tails. I did not let my gaze linger too long on any of the beasts, lest some fearsome sight should totally destroy my resolve. Besides, I thought it impolite to stare.

"Only one?" The Griffin stared down at me from the raised platform. "Only one deigns to come to our meeting. Well, I suppose it will be all right." The Griffin paused. "If you brought some gold."

"Pop!" The Hippogriff picked me up in its enormous beak and tossed me onto the platform. "Is that any way to treat a guest?"

"Excuse me," the Griffin said as I stood and brushed myself off. "Every so often, my upstart offspring makes a valid point. All this gold business—well, you know how it is with us mythological beasts, when instinct rears its ugly head. We haven't had much direct, one-on-one contact with humans before. But we mean to change that now."

"I've had direct contact with humans before!" a voice called from the audience. "Straight down the gullet to my stomach!"

There was laughter and shouting out in the crowd. Some seemed to be decrying the remark, saying things like, "Give the human a chance!" On the other hand, others were discussing just how much salt and oregano should be used to truly enhance my flavor. The group before me was, as my master might refer to them, a "rough audience." For the first time, I wished I had Ebenezum by my side to give me advice.

"They're a bit rowdy out there," the Griffin remarked. "We'll have to let them settle down. This is something of a convention, you know."

"Indeed," I said. I thought that if I could control my breathing, at least I could appear calm.

"Yes," the Griffin continued. "You should be very honored. You are the first human ever to attend a meeting of the Association for the Advancement of Mythical and Imaginary Beasts and Creatures. Or, as we like to call it, AFTAOMAIBAC.''

The Griffin turned to me, its eagle eyes piercing in their intensity. "Before we address the meeting, however, you and I are going to have a little talk."

"Indeed?" Instinctively, I backed toward the corner of the platform. It took an effort of will to keep my feet from going any farther.

It was all or nothing. I cleared my throat. Ebenezum wasn't here and I had to fill his shoes. I had to persevere, for my master, and Vushta!

"Be careful, sirrah!" I said in my best deep voice. "You are dealing with a wizard!"

"Why, yes, that's our point now." The Griffin's lion claws brushed against my feet. Its eagle breath was hot against my face. It smelled as though it had been eating rodents.

"We know we're dealing with a wizard," the Griffin continued. "But we're wondering why he didn't show up this morning?"

So I would have to go through all this again.

"Oh," I said nonchalantly. "You mean the old man. He may look like a wizard, that's true, but—" I waved the rest of the sentence away impatiently. "I've already explained this to your son!"

"Yeah, Pop, it's true!" the Hippogriff volunteered. "This guy says the old geezer used to be a great wizard, but now is a little gone in the head, you know?"

"But," the Griffin objected, "he was wearing wizard's robes—"

"Yeah, but no hat. Only real, full-time wizards can have hats!"

The Griffin turned to me. "Well, where is your hat, then, wizard?"

"Oh, Pop, you know how the Rok is. He lost it on the trip over here!"

The Griffin nodded grimly. "Have to have a talk with that Rok. Always losing things. Very well. You'll have a chance to prove your wizardly prowess a little later on. I still don't know about this older wizard. Would a retired human so desperately hold on to his old robes?"

"I'd believe it in a snap," the Hippogriff replied. "I know how stubborn certain mythological beasts can be when they get older."

"I beg your pardon!" There was battle lust in the Griffin's eyes. "Kindly explain to me, young beast, exactly what you mean—"

"Pop—" The Hippogriff waved its beak at the crowd. "The meeting?"

"Yes. Ahem. I forget my priorities." The Griffin shot me a final, withering glance. "This is the most important day of your life. Let us pray it is not your last."

"Pop!"

"Sorry. Old habits die hard. We are rewriting history here, and you will be a part of it." The Griffin reached out a comradely wing in my direction. "No longer will you be a mere human, forced to eke out a common destiny in the mud."

"Mere human?" How would my master handle this? I had stood here and listened to this beast go on for far too long. To make this work, I needed to adopt a truly wizardly manner. "I have told you, sirrah, I am skilled in the sorcerous arts."

"I'm sorry. You look much more skilled at carrying buckets and cleaning out cow stalls. That older fellow, now . . ."

I started to object, and found a lion's paw entwined with my shirt. The Griffin spoke very quietly:

"I will accept the fact that you have no gold. Lies are another matter entirely."

The Griffin turned to the assemblage.

"Brothers, sisters, and indeterminates! We are gathered here today to write a new page in mythology! Too long have we taken a back seat to dragons and unicorns, giants and Fairies! From this day forward, Griffins and Centaurs, Harpies and Satyrs will be on the tip of every tongue, and find a place in every heart!"

"And us Chimeras! Don't forget us Chimeras!"

"And what about us Kelpies!"

"How about us Nixies?"

"Yes! Yes!" the Griffin shouted above the crowd. "Chimeras, Kelpies, Nixies, everybody! We'll force mythology down their throats!"

The crowd went wild. They shouted some word, over and over. I strained to make it out.

A voice, much louder than the rest, called from the edge of the clearing:

"But nothing for Bog Womblers?"

The Griffin stopped, openmouthed.

"Bog Womblers?"

A large, gray thing sitting by the river raised its pseudopod. "Yes! Everyone forgets the Bog Womblers!"

"Yes, of course," the Griffin said, recovering rapidly. "Uh—Pookas, and Sphinxes, and Bog Womblers, too!"

The crowd went wilder.

"Uh, Pop?" the Hippogriff said softly.

The other beast glanced back irritably. "Yes, what is it now?"

The youngster nodded its head toward the far edge of

the clearing, beyond the Bog Wombler, where a number of near-naked women were wheeling carts into the crowd.

"Just that the refreshments are here."

"Is it that time already?" The Griffin shook its head angrily. "I've spent far too much time with this—human here! And I was just hitting my stride!"

It turned back to the assembled monsters. "Fellow mythical beasts! I know how deeply we all want to complete the business at hand. But our minds won't be at their best if our stomachs are empty, will they?"

The Griffin's remarks brought on a new chorus of shouts from the crowd. A couple of the larger creatures smiled my way. I was not sure if their large, toothsome grins and repeated licking of chops were all in all a sign of friendly good fellowship.

"Nymphs!" the Griffin called. "Bring on the refreshments!"

I was startled for an instant. The beasts were going to take a momentary pause in their strange ritual to refresh themselves. This could be just the chance I needed. Maybe I could discern what was really happening here, and what was expected of me. Maybe I could escape, and take Ebenezum with me. I looked around the dais on which we stood, but could see no gap in the tightly packed monsters.

The Griffin strode up to me on muscular cat feet. "Human. You have a few minutes to yourself. Step down and get to know some of our membership, if you will. We want to put you at your ease."

At my ease? Perhaps, I thought, I was needlessly worried. Perhaps this Griffin was merely a slightly overbearing father figure, and I was here to spread the news about this ritual back among humankind. Perhaps

I imagined things, and half the crowd did not fantasize about how I would taste in a light cream sauce. I did my best to smile at the Griffin in a comradely way.

"Oh," the Griffin added as an afterthought, "and after this break, you will have your chance to prove your mystic powers to the assembly."

SEVEN

A wizard's reputation is his bond, or so the sages say. And, as all learned men know, a reputation is difficult to build, and all too easily besmirched. The wizard with a fallen reputation is often led to less savory forms of employ, and, while these sometimes pay better than whatever the wizard was doing before, they are not the sort of thing one writes home to Mother about. The successful wizard, therefore, should develop three or four reputations simultaneously, and then, happily, will have one for every occasion.

—THE TEACHINGS OF EBENEZUM,
VOLUME XIII

Perhaps, on the other hand, escape was a very good idea. I looked again, out over the multitude of monsters. A dozen scantily clad women were pushing large wooden carts through the crowd. The carts appeared to be refreshment wagons, filled with large kegs of mead, trays full of biscuits and small sandwiches, and little, squirmy things that squealed loudly when the creatures swallowed them.

I could but hope that if they ate those things, they would be less hungry for me. There was nothing for it but to go out amidst the crowd.

"Hey! It's the human!"

I was already attracting notice.

"Do you think he's a wizard?"

There was a coarse laugh. "Sure, and I'm a Pooka!"

"Wait a second. I thought you *were* a Pooka!"

"No, I'm a Nix! Good heavens, don't you have any eyes in that Chimera head of yours?"

"What do you mean? I'm not a Chimera!"

I lost track of the conversation when one of the voluptuously attractive, and nearly naked, women stood before me.

"Hello, big boy," she said huskily.

"Why—um," I replied. She took my hand as I spoke. Her pink tongue moved slowly across her white teeth.

"Would you like a little something?" the husky voice asked.

"Why—um," I replied. I seemed to have broken into a heavy sweat. I did not realize the day was so warm.

"Hey! Keep your hands off our Nymphs!" A short fellow with a pointy beard stared angrily at me.

"Who are you?" I had the awful feeling that a wizard would know more about mythical beasts than I did. What little I had learned came from conversations with Hubert, a dragon of my acquaintance who was pursuing a career in vaudeville. And Hubert hadn't talked at all about short fellows with pointy beards.

"Get a load of this guy!" The pointy-bearded fellow, who also appeared to have hooves and a tail, sneered. "You know what a Satyr is, don't you?"

Oh. I was on safe ground now. This was something I *had* discussed with Hubert. "Sure," I replied. "That's a form of comedy, right?"

"Who is this guy?" The bearded fellow searched the heavens above us. "No. Satyr. S-A-T-Y-R! You know, the pipes of Pan! Frolicking and disporting with Nymphs among the spring flowers! That sort of thing!"

"Why, certainly." I dismissed my foolish error with a wave of my wizardly hand. "Now that you say so, of course. It's just that I have a few things on my mind. . . ."

"And your mind is where they're going to stay!" The Satyr glanced at the nearly naked Nymph. "Scoot, Nymphie. We'll do some frollicking and disporting later on, okay?"

The Nymph showed me a final smile.

"Maybe I can get you something sometime, big boy." Her voice, if anything, was lower and huskier than before.

"Why—um," I replied as I watched her retreat through the crowd.

"You keep shaking your head like that, you'll get sick," a deep voice said nearby. I looked up to see a massive wall of gray flesh. "Us Bog Womblers know all about sick."

So I had made my way through the throng to the Bog Wombler. That meant I was almost to the edge of the clearing. Perhaps I could escape after all.

"Indeed," I replied, doing my best to act wizardly. "Here I am, taking a stroll, to get some air."

"Not a bad idea, with that crowd," the huge creature intoned. "Bog Womblers don't like crowds."

"Indeed," I stated.

"There's a stream just behind me. You might want to refresh yourself. If we don't have a stream around, we Bog Womblers are in big trouble."

"Indeed?" I answered, barely able to contain my elation. A stream? I wondered if any of the creatures came by boat. My escape was beginning to seem more possible with every passing minute.

Still, I shouldn't appear too eager. I would engage in small talk for an instant, then saunter away.

"Pardon me," I said, "but I don't know what a Bog Wombler does."

"You're not alone. No one ever knows." It paused and sighed, fixing me with a single, bloodshot eye.

"We womble," it said at last.

"Oh," I replied. "Indeed. How interesting. I think I'll go and get that drink you suggested. Awfully nice meeting you."

I skirted the Bog Wombler and headed for freedom.

The stream was not as deserted as I had hoped. Another two dozen strange creatures, many with extremely fishy characteristics, lounged in and about the water. Possibly, if I were to wander downstream a bit . . . I gave a wide berth to the nastier-looking fish-things. With some reluctance, I passed the Mermaids by without a second glance.

The trees grew larger and thicker as I walked downstream, which suited my purpose perfectly. No one had tried to stop me. Even if I couldn't find a boat, the foliage might give me sufficient cover to escape on foot.

Somehow, though, I would have to double back and rescue my master. And while I might be able to move quickly through the forest for hours on end, I doubted if the wizard was yet up to it. For that reason alone, a boat would be very useful.

I came to a bend in the stream. There, moored in the shallows, was a canoe.

My luck got better with every passing moment! At this rate, Ebenezum and I would be well on our way to Vushta by nightfall.

The boat was tied by a line to a sturdy oak. It took me a moment to undo the knot, fiendishly tied, I imagined, by some hands that were not quite human. I gave a muted cry of satisfaction as the final strand pulled free. Now I would push the canoe silently downstream, and hide it somewhere to avoid detection until I had rescued Ebenezum and brought him back to the craft.

I squatted to push the canoe fully into the water.

The canoe didn't move.

Something was keeping it from moving. I now took note of the fact that the boat seemed to contain a horse's hoof.

"Hi there," the Hippogriff said.

Panic struck me. Clearly it was time for a change of plans.

"Well, excuse me!" I cried, doing my best to conjure up wizardly indignation. "It appears I can't have any privacy at all! I'll have you know that even we wizards have certain bodily functions that we have to take care of."

"In a boat?" The Hippogriff shook its eagle beak. "Guess you'll just have to hold it in now, won't you? It's time for the meeting to begin."

The beast looked aloft and whistled. "Oh, Rok!"

There was a great fluttering of wings.

The Hippogriff fixed me again with its eagle stare. "You've been a naughty human, wandering away like that when we needed your wizardly skill. But you're the guest of honor. Spare no expense, right? So we'll get you an express ride back to the podium."

Something very large landed next to me.

"Hey," the huge bird drawled. "What's happening?"

"Got another job for you, Rok," the Hippogriff

said. "We need to get this guy back to the podium in a hurry."

"Hey," the Rok replied. "That's cool."

"And, Rok?" the Hippogriff said somewhat tentatively. "I've got a request from my father, the Griffin? It seems you dropped some of this fellow's things last time you carried him. My pop was wondering if you'd kind of be a little more careful?"

The huge bird focused its eyes for the first time. It glared at the Hippogriff. "Hey, horse, I got big claws. Sometimes things slip away. Sometimes they don't." It flexed a claw idly, crushing a tree. "Dig?"

This was terrible. There had to be some way that I could get away.

"Excuse me?" I asked, trying to sound a bit more humble than before. "I really could use a bush somewhere."

"You should have thought of that earlier," the Hippogriff replied. "Now, it's showtime!"

The Rok's claws surrounded me.

"Listen, if it gets really bad," the Hippogriff added, "there's a crawl space under the stage."

The beast waved its wing as the Rok carried me aloft.

"Nothing is too good for our guests!" were the last words I heard before the Hippogriff, too, took flight.

The crowd didn't seem to notice us passing overhead. I heard snatches of conversation as I flew by.

"Would you stop changing your shape every two minutes? It's very difficult to concentrate—"

"How can I tell you're the Sphinx?"

"How about a riddle? I've got a million of them. What's yellow, has four wings, weighs two thousand pounds and goes—"

I had grabbed on to the claws and had a much better view than the first time I'd traveled this way. That's how I managed to see something out of the corner of my eye. Something dark and fast-moving, and maybe as big as the Rok. It was too high in the sky to tell. Maybe what it was was something that hadn't been invited to this convention. Whatever that could possibly be . . .

The Rok deposited me on the dirt by the stage. The Hippogriff landed nearby.

"About time you got back," the Griffin growled. It removed its claws from where it had been shredding a corner of the stage.

"Pop, I think I saw—" the Hippogriff began worriedly.

"Here we are"—the Griffin cut the youngster off—"at the most important moment ever in the history of mythological beastdom, and you two are galavanting around. Don't give a thought to the old Griffin, oh no. I'm merely the one running the show. Who cares if I'm kept informed?"

The Griffin leapt six feet straight into the air, grabbing a small bird in its beak. It crashed back onto the stage, crunching and swallowing noisily.

"Haven't even had time for a decent meal," it mumbled.

There might be a way out of this yet. Perhaps I could get on this beast's good side. If it had a good side.

"Indeed," I said, "the weight of responsibility upon you must be terrible."

The Griffin nodded solemnly.

"How did they pick you to be the leader, if I might inquire?"

"Quiet down out there!" The Griffin raked its claws through the air so fast it made the wind sing. The crowd got considerably quieter. "Oh, I know exactly how to deal with creatures. I always thought it was my Griffin's keen sense of humor and personal style. Keep them laughing, that's what I always say." It raised its voice to the crowd again. "Are you going to be quiet out there, or is there going to be trouble?"

The crowd got quieter still. "You're to be commended," I added. "You've really gathered quite a variety of creatures."

"Yep, got almost everybody," the Griffin replied. "We're still waiting for the Phoenix. He keeps promising to show up."

Could that be what I saw? A Phoenix? Then why wasn't he here?

The Griffin looked wistfully at the sky. "You'd think there'd be more birds. I don't work well on an empty stomach. Oh well, it can't be helped." The beast sighed. "We have history to make."

"Fellow mythological beasts!" The Griffin's voice rang out over the throng. " 'Tis the time for decision! Bring out the unicorn!"

The crowd began to chant the phrase that had puzzled me before. It sounded like "Half-past three! Half-past three!" Was someone keeping track of the time?

"Yes, that's right!" the Griffin continued. "This is our moment in history. No longer will we have to take a back seat to unicorns, dragons and the like. We're here to see that we get our fair share of tapestry space!"

The crowd was on its feet, or wings, or fins, or, in the case of the Bog Wombler, whatever.

"That's right, mythical beasts! Our fair share of tapestry space! And a maiden for every monster!"

The crowd was at it again. "Tap-es-try!" they called. "Tapestry! Tapestry!"

Oh, that was it then. Tapestry. Quite simple, really.

Hoots of derision rose from the audience. The Hippogriff was leading in the unicorn.

"Here, then," the Griffin was saying, "is our chief competition."

Shouts of "Nyah-nyah-nyah!" and "Who's the walking hat rack?" followed the unicorn through the crowd. Somehow, the magnificent beast seemed above it all.

"Now, what has this beast got that we don't have?" the Griffin asked. "A golden horn perhaps. A magnificent coat, maybe, a stately bearing? Even—hah!—a way with virgins? Not enough, I say! Why are tapestries so crowded with unicorns? How come dragons have cornered the damsel-in-distress market? It sets a mythological beast to thinking, let me tell you!"

The Griffin waved a wing grandly in my direction. "That's why we invited a wizard here today. True, he may not be much of a wizard, but we're operating on very short notice. Still, we are here to show the wizard the wisdom of our course, and to let him use his magic to spread the word!"

A voice came from the crowd. "Then can we eat him?"

"Only if he doesn't do his job!" The Griffin made a short, barking sound that might have been a laugh. "But all kidding aside, fellow creatures! No longer will maidens flock solely to unicorns and dragons! Once we're done, every Kobold and Hob and Fruich among you will have a dozen tapestries, and maidens beating down your door!"

"Tap-es-try!" the crowd chanted. "Tap-es-try!"

A mournful voice cut through the melee.

"What about us Bog Womblers?"

"Bog Womblers, too! When we are done, every Bog Wombler will be covered with maidens!"

That many maidens? It was an awesome thought. From the size of the thing, I would guess a Bog

Wombler would take up a tapestry all by itself.

"How about Satyrs?" somebody cried. "Satyrs already get maidens!"

One of the pointy-bearded fellows jumped forward. "We do not! We get Nymphs. It's another thing altogether. You have to spend all your time chasing them around the forest." The fellow shook his fists with frustration. "And have you ever tried to have an intelligent conversation with a Nymph? All they want to talk about is the weather and flower arrangements!"

"Yes, yes!" the Griffin agreed. "Maidens for everyone!" The beast turned to me. "Are you ready?"

I cleared my throat. "Indeed?" I managed. "Ready for what?"

"For the big moment, of course. Oh. We haven't explained that, have we? So much to do, so little time. You'll forgive me for not telling you this before, won't you? That's a good human."

"Now wait a minute!" I shouted. "You get a big bird to drag me and my master to this place, plop me down in a leaky, drafty shack, throw me out here without any breakfast, and expect me to perform for everybody? I will do no such thing!"

They had finally done it. I was angry.

"Hmm," the Griffin mused. "Perhaps this fellow is a wizard after all." The beast turned to the Hippogriff. "Son, see if you can find some—oh, whatever it is humans eat!"

"Sure, Pop!" The Hippogriff galloped off the stage.

The Griffin turned back to me. "Now that we have addressed your needs, we can get down to business.

"Fellow mythological creatures! Our guest, the wizard, has asked for a few minutes to prepare his spells before he broadcasts our message to wizards everywhere. A reasonable request, I think, and one that will give him a chance to hear more about our noble purpose!"

Shouts of "Yeah, wizard! That's tellin' him!" and "Let's eat the unicorn!" drifted in from the crowd.

"In the meantime," the Griffin continued, "I will explore some of the finer points of our seventy-two demands, to be presented to all of humanity, as well as the world below."

The world below? Was this creature talking about the Netherhells? Now that I thought of it, I remembered Ebenezum once telling me that magical beasts were only partially of this world, and partially Netherhells-inspired. That meant they might have connections who would know the Netherhells' fiendish plots!

"You're talking about the Netherhells!" I interrupted loudly.

The Griffin paused in its oratory.

"Yes?"

"But the demons have concocted some fantastic scheme to rule the world above ground, too!"

"Oh, yes, of course," the Griffin said. "We know all about that."

"You know what the Netherhells intend?" I cried. "You have to tell me!"

"Sorry." The Griffin shook its head. "We have an understanding with the Netherhells. They're fantastic creatures, too, you know. Besides, it would hurt our bargaining position."

I started to object, when the Hippogriff galloped back on the stage. The creature dropped a bundle at my feet.

"Sorry, fella," the beast said. "Best I could do on short notice."

The bundle was moving and making mewling noises.

"No time to cook anything, I'm afraid." The Hippogriff shrugged its wings.

I decided not to look inside. "Indeed," I muttered. "I'll eat it later."

"Fellow creatures!" The Griffin had returned to its oratory. For the moment, I had lost my chance. My mind raced. What could these strange creatures know about the foul schemes of the Netherhells? And how could I get them to talk?

"The time has come," the Griffin continued, "to promote ourselves before the unlearned masses. 'Tis a sad fact that Sphinxes and Hippogriffs rarely crop up in everyday conversation. Hobs and Kobolds are talked about even less. We are going to change all that!"

Some members of the crowd cheered.

"Our first order of business today is to devise phrases that will help the unwashed masses identify us. I will give you an example:

"If one of the masses should describe something as 'As lovely as a unicorn,' or 'As deadly as a dragon,' no one hearing them would think twice. They know all about unicorns and dragons. They see them on tapestries. They're constantly having to go out and rescue maidens from their clutches! Unicorns and dragons are a part of their everyday lives!

"But what of Chimeras and Centaurs? I have gone up to a member of the unwashed and said that word—'Chimera!' And what did they say to me? I'll tell you! They said '*Gesundheit!*'

"Let me assure you, this is a situation we can no longer tolerate. If unicorns and dragons are known by their slogans, the rest of us will have slogans as well!"

Now the crowd went wild.

The Hippogriff brought the unicorn up onto the stage.

The Griffin glanced at the brilliant white creature with the golden horn. "I brought this unicorn before us for a purpose. We can look at this beast and know that it is no better than any of us."

The unicorn snorted and shook its magnificently flowing mane. Taut muscles rippled beneath its perfect coat. Its golden horn glinted in the sun.

"Well," the Griffin added, "perhaps it is a little better than some of us, but I'm sure that we all have hidden attributes that a unicorn couldn't even dream of!"

The Griffin spread its wings. "All right now! We need to start somewhere, and I have decided that I shall volunteer, to demonstrate one approach we might take. To begin, I look down upon my physical form, and catalogue my various positive features."

The creature flapped its wings with slow majesty. It brought a welcome breeze to the platform. Whatever was in the sack the Hippogriff had brought me was starting to smell.

"First, I have the wings and head of the great eagle, predator of the skies!"

The Griffin then roared and waved a lion's claw with talons extended. It seemed to be getting somewhat carried away. I took a step back for safety's sake.

"Next, I have the body of the mighty lion, king of the beasts!"

The tail that looked like half a snake whipped across the stage, knocking my intended lunch out into the crowd. At least now, I hoped, I would not be expected to eat it. Politeness or no, there are certain limits even a wizard's apprentice has to observe.

"Lastly, but no less mighty, is my serpent's tail,

powerful enough to crush the life from half the creatures of the forest.''

The Griffin paused for dramatic effect. ''What does this all indicate? Yes, yes, I can feel you thinking it! Nobility. Therefore, we will add one phrase to the common speech: 'As noble as a Griffin!' ''

The Griffin shot a look at the unicorn, who had snorted at an inappropriate moment, then turned back to the crowd.

''There, you see how easy it is? All right. Who's next?''

The pointy-bearded fellow in the front row waved his triangular-shaped whistle. ''What about Satyrs?''

''Satyrs already get maidens!'' somebody insisted.

''I'm sorry,'' the Griffin interjected. ''Maidens were dealt with earlier on the agenda. Yes, what about Satyrs? We need a slogan to make you, too, a common, household name.''

''Say, Pop!'' the Hippogriff called. ''Try 'As sly as a Satyr.' ''

The Griffin considered it. He glanced at the fellow with the pointy beard, who appeared to be frowning.

''No, no, that has some negative connotations, doesn't it? Maybe 'As sexy as a Satyr'?''

The pointy-bearded fellow shifted uncomfortably. He cleared his throat. ''Please, we're trying to downplay certain aspects of our image.''

''Very well,'' the Griffin said impatiently. ''Do you have any suggestions?''

''Yes!'' The fellow smiled. ''I have catalogued my body parts as you did, and I've come up with a phrase that's ideal!'' He cleared his throat again.

''As noble as a Satyr!''

The crowd applauded enthusiastically.

''Oh. Yes. I see,'' the Griffin murmured. ''Well,

then, 'As noble as a Satyr' it will be!''

The motion was passed to popular acclaim.

A mournful voice came from the audience.

"What about us Bog Womblers?"

"Bog Womblers?" the Hippogriff muttered.

"Simple, but effective!" the Griffin cried, stepping forward. "As noble as a Bog Wombler!"

The crowd went wild.

The Griffin turned to the Hippogriff. "This is not going quite as well as I had hoped. 'Tis time for the wizard."

It took me a second to realize that they meant me. I had quite forgotten, what with the grand sweep of oratory going on before me, that I was supposed to prepare myself for my task.

The Griffin turned to me. "Come now and prove your sorcerous skills. Spread the word about AFTAO-MAIBAC to wizards throughout the world!"

"Pardon me," I said, "but I'm not sure my magic works that way."

The Griffin grumbled deep in its throat. It fixed me again with its eagle eye.

"I, and the collective beasts of our brotherhood, have been lenient, considering your situation, but I am afraid our patience is almost spent. It is time to make our organization known to the world!"

"If not, of course," the Hippogriff added in a more reasonable tone, "there are those among us who would be glad to eat you."

"Yeah!" someone called from the audience. "Waste not, want not!"

"Come now," the Griffin reproached. "You've spent far too long in your preparation. 'Tis time to prove your mettle."

The beast turned to the throng. "Come, fellow creatures! Let us cheer the wizard on. Soon, every sorcerer will know our name! AFTAOMAIBAC! AFTAO-MAIBAC! AFTAOMAIBAC!''

A ragged cheer arose from the crowd as they attempted to repeat the group's name.

So I would be eaten at last. Unless—could I dare hope? There was one thing that might work. What if I contacted Norei and somehow got her to speak through me to the assemblage? I could then convince the magical beasts that I had spoken with another sorcerer. Yes! I had to talk with Norei again, anyway! It was a brilliant stroke. Maybe I would survive this after all.

I began to think of grackles.

"AFTAOMAIBAC! AFTAOMAIBAC!"

It was hard to concentrate with the cheering of the crowd. I looked at the Griffin, leading the throng. Its serpent tail whipped fearsomely back and forth in time with the cheers, as its lion's claws ripped boards from the platform and tossed them amidst the crowd. Its eagle beak turned to regard me.

My grackle thoughts went flying aloft.

Norei! I called. Norei!

"Wuntvor? Is it you?"

I saw her below me, marching across an open field. My grackle thoughts flew swiftly to her side.

Yes, my red-haired beauty. Yes! I need your help desperately!

"Oh," she said with a certain amount of disdain, "and about time. So you've finally come back to learn the fate the Netherhells have planned for your master?"

Yes, uh, and no! I admitted. You see, there's this large group of monsters—

"Monsters? There's no time for that now, Wuntvor. I fear the Netherhells suspect our communication. You have used this spell too openly, and too many times. I feel the demons are taking steps against us, even as we speak.''

My grackle form cried in alarm: We must talk hurriedly, then, my love. I need a sign from you, if I am to retain my life. You see, I've found myself captured by this convention of mythological beasts—

"Convention of what? Wuntvor! Sometimes your playfulness can be very inappropriate! Listen now to what I have to say. I fear the Netherhells will come between us, and we will never have a chance—"

My beloved screamed. I could no longer see her.

Another face swam before my eyes. A demonic face, with many, many teeth.

With a start, I realized it was Guxx Unfufadoo, the dread, rhyming demon who was the cause of my master's malady.

"We've had enough of your pitiful spell,
For the time has come for your death knell!"

I heard myself scream. I blinked, and found I was back among the monsters.

"So," the Griffin said, sharpening its claws on the remains of the stage. "When do you begin your spell?"

There was a massive explosion.

"Heads up, kiddies!" a high voice cried. "It's Brownie time!"

The smoke set me to coughing. Through watery eyes, I saw that two things had materialized near me on the stage. One was the Brownie.

The other was the largest shoe that I had ever seen.

EIGHT

Wizards encounter periods of crisis from time to time. It comes with the job, right along with the robes and the pointy hat. Now, some wizards thrive on crisis, and there is quite a bit of gold to be made, should the magician survive, by thrusting oneself into the thick of things. The more experienced mage, however, makes ample use of soothsaying spells, so that he may collect the monies, reassure the populace, and still have time to leave the area before the thick of things arrives.

— *THE TEACHINGS OF EBENEZUM,*
VOLUME IV

The shoe spoke to me.

"Wuntvor! 'Tis I!"

It was my master's voice! My first thought was that the Brownie had somehow transformed my master into a giant shoe. After a moment, I regained my wits, however, and realized that the shoe had been built large enough to house Ebenezum. And now he was here, by my side, in the midst of all this magic, and he was not sneezing!

"Master!" I cried joyfully. "You are cured!"

"In a manner of speaking," Ebenezum replied dryly. " 'Tis only a matter of my spending the rest of my life inside a shoe."

"But how did you get here?" I asked.

"Through Brownie magic, apparently. It all started when our Brownie showed up at the shack where I was resting. He'd brought this other little fellow along that he kept calling 'Your Brownieship'—" The wizard paused. "But what's going on here? It's hard for me to see through the buttonholes."

"Well, this is a convention of mythological beasts," I began hastily. "And they wanted me to contact another wizard, or they were going to eat me, and—"

"Who dares to disturb the first regularly scheduled meeting of the Association for the Advancement of Mythical and Imaginary Beasts and Creatures?" the Griffin interrupted with a roar. "A talking shoe?"

"Careful, Pop," the Hippogriff chided. "He may be eligible for membership."

The Brownie walked up to me, all smiles.

"Is this a wish or what?" he said proudly. "We Brownies are new to this game, but once we get going—"

"Would an enchanted shoe be mythological?" The Griffin glared at its offspring. "I'll have to check the bylaws."

The leader of the beasts coughed and turned to us. "One thing I do know, however. Fairies are definitely not welcome at our gatherings!"

"Fairies!" the Brownie cried. "Fairies! Could a Fairy do this?"

The little fellow closed his eyes and shuffled his feet.

The shoe floated in the air for a minute, then returned to the stage with a resounding crash.

"Indeed," the wizard's voice came from deep within the leather. "If I might make a suggestion—"

"Little enough magic! A Griffin could move that shoe with even less effort!"

"Please," the wizard began again. "If you might just hear me out—"

The Griffin's tail slithered under the shoe, tossing it two feet in the air. It fell to the stage with an even louder crash.

"Enough!" the wizard called from within. A single, dark-robed hand emerged from inside the shoe leather. A lightning bolt shot down from the sky, searing the space midway between Griffin and Brownie.

"Oh wow!" the Hippogriff exclaimed. "Yes, I think the enchanted shoe has an excellent case for immediate membership."

"If you will listen to me now?" Ebenezum's muffled voice remarked.

"Listen up!" the Hippogriff shouted. "The enchanted shoe has the floor!"

"Very well. First, let me say that this little fellow here is not a Fairy at all. He is, rather, very much a Brownie."

"Really?" the Hippogriff interjected. "You know, Brownies could be eligible for membership, too."

The Brownie thanked my master.

"Don't mention it. Indeed, 'twas the least I could do. Second, I am more than what I seem. Rather than being an enchanted shoe, I am a wizard in disguise!"

The crowd roared in surprise.

"I see." The Griffin had gotten over its shock at almost being singed, and had stepped forward to once again take control. "It's a shame, really. An enchanted shoe would have made such a colorful member. But Brownies now, there's an awful lot of you, aren't there? You know, of course, that there's an entrance fee. And then there're the annual dues. But, what a membership can do for you!"

"Your pardon," the wizard said. "I am not done speaking."

Everyone was silent. I marveled at what a lightning bolt could do for crowd control.

"I am a great wizard," Ebenezum said, "called by my compatriot here to—" My master paused. I had not been able to tell him any more of my plight! "—to do whatever I have been called here to do!" he finished majestically. Somehow, coming from his mouth, the words all made sense.

"Doom!" A voice carried from the edge of the silent crowd.

The Griffin ignored it. "So this fellow really is a wizard after all? I tell you, they must have simplified the entrance exam since I was a hatchling." The beast paused, glanced at the sky, and flapped its wings defensively. "Sorry! Just voicing my opinion. I'm sure I know as little about wizards as wizards know about Griffins!"

Ebenezum's hand emerged from the shoe again.

"Not to say that wizards lack knowledge—"

"Pop!" the Hippogriff whispered. "Get a hold of yourself! We're supposed to tell the wizards our demands!"

The wizard's hand felt about for another buttonhole and extracted a cloth from it. The hand disappeared within the shoe again. I heard the faint sound of a nose being blown.

"I know exactly what I'm doing!" the Griffin snapped. "That's the problem with youngsters today.

No sense of diplomacy. And the things they bring home to clutter the nest. And their taste in music! You know what this teenager likes? Madrigals!'' The Griffin groaned in agony. "Give me a good old Gregorian chant any day!''

The Griffin walked over to the shoe and stared straight into a buttonhole. "But let's put that aside. We all want to work together. Let me show you our list of seventy-three proposals. Of special interest is our suggestion for a joint wizard and mythological beast steering committee. Of course, we'll need to receive some modest funds to get it going. Think of it as an act of good faith on the part of wizards everywhere.''

The Griffin paused and looked out to the crowd. There was quite a commotion in the middle of the audience. I made out an occasional "Doom!" amid the hubbub.

"Look here!" called a voice so grating that it only could be Snarks. "No one's eating anybody else here. And no animal with the head of a chicken is going to tell me anything!''

The noise rose considerably. I thought I heard sounds of genuine conflict.

"Indeed,'' said the wizard within his shoe. "Do you think your fellow creatures could stop molesting the newcomers? I would like to see those two up here with us.'' A hand emerged casually from the shoe, as if to test the temperature of the air.

"Most certainly!" The Griffin laughed its barking laugh, as if this were all great fun among old cronies, then turned and gave instructions to the crowd to let the strangers pass.

"Doom,'' Hendrek said when he arrived on the stage. "We have come to save you.''

Snarks peered at the Griffin. "Look here! *Another*

creature with a chicken head!"

The Griffin was speechless. Its tail whipped about as if it were looking for something to strangle. Snarks, for the moment at least, was standing out of reach.

"You know," Snarks went on, "I've noticed that a lot of the creatures around here have an attitude problem." He paused to survey the crowd. "Well, I suppose when you look like you've been put together from spare parts in somebody's tool shed, there's bound to be difficulty. Still, if I had a brief talk with them, I'm sure I could straighten them out. I have Netherhells experience, you know!"

"If you were not under the protection of a wizard—" The Griffin became too choked with emotion to continue.

"And the wizard's under my protection as well," Snarks added happily. "For I can see the truth, wherever it may hide. There seems to be little enough of it around here at the moment."

"Doom." Hendrek moved to Snarks's side. Headbasher swung free in the large warrior's hand.

The truth-telling demon waved at the warrior. "Never fear, friend Hendrek. We have the upper hand here. Compared to all these creatures, you look positively normal!"

"So what do we do now?" Hendrek turned to me. "We have come to rescue you from fiends unknown."

"Wait a sec," the Hippogriff cut in. "Rescue him from what? I'll have you know that this is the first annual meeting of a very important new bestiary interest group!"

"Like the man said," Snarks chimed in, "we've come to rescue you from fiends unknown." The demon looked down at the crowd of mythological animals, who seemed to be growing more and more restive as the drama played itself out onstage. "And not a moment too soon, either!"

"Excuse me," the wizard intoned from his leathery depths. "While I am sure we could go on exchanging pleasantries all day, there are matters we must attend to. Let us finish our business here quickly and be on our way."

"Certainly." The Griffin ruffled its feathers in an attempt to regain composure. "We mythological animals don't ask for much. We only want to gain the stature in society that rightfully belongs to us. It will be so easy! We've made up some tapestry design guidelines that will revolutionize the industry. And I think we've been more than reasonable in our maiden-allotment quotas."

"Indeed," the wizard said. "And exactly what is it that you want wizards to do?"

"Why, the same things wizards always do! Make things happen." The Griffin sidled even closer to the shoe. "Listen, we're not fooled by traditional power structures. After all, we're mythological. That, to say the least, gives one a unique perspective. We know, with all the kings and mayors and knights and town councilmen around, things only get done when a wizard steps in. In fact, the higher the king/mayor/knight/town councilman to wizard ratio in a certain area, the longer it takes anyone to do anything!" The beast's voice dropped to a whisper. "Besides that, there also seems to be a lot of money around wizards."

The Griffin paused, but the shoe made no reply.

"All right. So we want to talk business. It is not enough that all but a few haughty mythological beasts have joined together to make a statement of purpose. We need wizards to spread the word. Other humans listen to wizards. They know that if they don't, bad things just might happen to them. And that's just the kind of spokespeople my organization needs!''

"Then you're speaking of a cooperative agreement?"
I thought I noted some interest in Ebenezum's muffled
voice.

"Well, eventually, there will be money involved," the
Griffin continued. "It's all part of our seventy-two
demands, which I'm sure you'll enjoy reading when you
have the time. Why, I imagine the tapestry royalties
alone will net us a small fortune—"

"Indeed. You used the word 'eventually.' Say
wizards do spread the word? What is the working
wizard to do for ready cash until that 'eventually' comes
about?"

"An old, established order such as the wizards—"
The Griffin paused ominously, doing its best to glare at
the shoe. I saw for the first time how my master's
leather covering might enhance his bargaining power.
The Griffin took a deep breath. "The least wizards can
do is make a voluntary contribution as a sign of good
will!"

"No," Ebenezum said slowly. "I think not."

The Griffin roared. "No one ever says no to us! We
are fearsome mythological beasts!"

"That is true," Ebenezum replied. "And I am a
wizard."

My chest swelled with pride at my master's bargaining
skill. The beasts were no match for him, even while he
was trapped in a shoe. As his apprentice, I knew that
there were many truths about my master, but one was
truer than all the rest:

No one fights Ebenezum over money matters and
wins.

"What say, guys?" Snarks's voice filled the ominous
silence. "Let's blow this zoo and get back on our way to

Vushta. If we stick around here much longer, we're bound to get fleas!''

The Griffin screamed in rage. The Hippogriff, somewhat more mildly, remarked: ''Mythological animals never have fleas.''

''Not even mythological fleas?'' Snarks rejoined. ''What's the matter, you not good enough for them? Come to think of it, from the way you look, I'd hate to imagine how you taste. Ugh. It's enough to put a demon off his lunch. And you should see what demons eat!''

''Friend Snarks,'' I cut in, ''perhaps it is time to resume our journey as you—''

The Griffin leapt to where Snarks had been standing only seconds before. The beast's claws shredded the floorboards.

''Not only ugly, but slow,'' Snarks added. ''If you're going to leap after me, you should lean back more on your haunches, you know. It'll give you more spring. And if you'd extend your claws the teeniest bit—''

The Griffin lunged again, overshooting the demon and flying completely off the stage.

I turned to the wizard. ''Master? What are we going to do?''

''Hey, is it time for another Brownie wish?''

The little fellow stood by my foot. In all the excitement, I had completely forgotten him.

''Yeah, you'll have to excuse me,'' the Brownie continued. ''I've just been standing here, admiring my handiwork. Here before us, the living embodiment of Brownie Power, and the first of what I am sure will be several successful wishes in my career. My only problem now is how do I top this?''

''Perhaps,'' the wizard said from deep within the shoe, ''you can find some way to get this shoe and the rest of us out of this place." The wizard's sneeze was muffled by the shoe as well.

"No problem at all!" the Brownie said as Snarks went sailing by, the Griffin in pursuit. "Give me a moment to get my wits about me. I'm still new at this, only one wish under my belt. And, incidentally, I won't be offended at all if anyone has any suggestions!"

He tapped on the shoe. "I did need some help before from His Brownieship to move this thing around. Maybe we could all get together and carry you? Of course, you and the shoe would be pretty heavy. We might need you to come out, too, to help support the load. Well, that wouldn't do, though, in the midst of all this magic, would it?" The Brownie fell to silent musing.

"You really shouldn't take offense at what I say!" Snarks panted, obviously out of breath. "I am but voicing my humble opinion on the appearance of your following. I'm sure they're dressed at the height of fashion for things made out of spare animal parts. And who are we to dictate fashion? Why, look at the warrior Hendrek, here. Did you ever see a more ugly belt than that checkered thing he's wearing?"

All the color drained from Hendrek's ruddy face.

"I have never worn a belt!" The warrior looked to his waist. "Doom!"

The belt slithered away from Hendrek's waist and assumed standard demon form. It was Brax, in its demonic checkered suit.

The warrior swung Headbasher far over his helmeted head.

"Fiend!" he intoned. "Must you forever plague me?"

"Oh, come on now, Hendy baby." The demon

smiled broadly as it dodged the warrior's wild swing. "What did I tell you about protecting my investment?"

The demon turned and looked out over the audience. "Hey there! I haven't seen such a large group of potential customers in my entire career. What, you think being uniquely magical creatures will be enough to see you through the coming conflict? Don't you believe it! You're going to need all the help you can get."

"Wait a moment!" the Griffin shouted. "Coming conflict? What coming conflict? We have an agreement with the Netherhells!"

"So you haven't heard!" the smiling demon chortled as it ducked another blow from the warclub. "On the day of the Forxnagel, all contracts are null and void!"

"The Forxnagel!" Ebenezum cried from within his shoe.

That's right! With all the excitement here, I had forgotten to tell my master what I had learned during my grackle spell.

"Wuntvor!" the wizard called.

I ran to his side and told him that Norei had confirmed this news.

"Indeed," Ebenezum murmured. "And me trapped within a shoe! We will have to find a way to convey my new home from place to place, even if we must carry it all the way to Vushta! Ask if they have any carts about."

"Carts?" the Hippogriff snorted. "What use have mythological beasts for carts when we have the wings of eagles and the hooves of stallions? Besides, I'm afraid we've never been very good at building wheels. It's the lack of thumbs, you know." The beast nodded toward its wings. "Guess you're out of luck."

"Yes, you're all out of luck!" Brax the salesdemon

cried. "But you might be able to extend your freedom, and perhaps even your miserable lives, for hours or perhaps even days if you own one of my enchanted weapons!"

"Doom," Hendrek muttered in my ear. "Extend our miserable lives? This new twist to the demon's sales talk does not bode well."

Brax indicated the larger warrior with a wave and a hop. "Just look at this satisfied customer! Why, if he does not fulfill his contract with the Netherhells now, he will complete it gladly, after we have won!"

"Doom!"

Headbasher went crashing through the stage.

"What a weapon!" Brax shook its head in admiration.

"It can't be," the Griffin repeated. "We have an understanding with the Netherhells."

"Griffins sometimes get set in their ways," the Hippogriff confided.

"Understandable," Snarks cried as he ran past. "It takes the beast so long to keep its body parts straight, it doesn't have time to think of anything else."

Snarks ran. The Griffin roared. Brax sold. Headbasher crashed. And my master sneezed again.

The situation had been merely out of hand before. Now it had degenerated into something completely beyond human comprehension. The shoe had seemed to shield my master up to a point. However, there was such a sorcerous overload hereabouts that even the Brownie's protection could not hold it back for long.

The world was falling apart around us. We had to escape. I only prayed we could reach Vushta in time.

But how could we carry my master?

My eyes wandered to the pen at the side of the stage.

The pen that contained the unicorn. That overmuscled beast had helped to get us into this situation. Perhaps it could help us out of it as well.

"What a mess!" the unicorn cried as I approached. In all the tumult, no one had even noticed my leaving the stage. "What do they want me here for? I'm supposed to be out frolicking through verdant fields!"

I knew exactly what they wanted the unicorn for. One look at this creature, and the mythological beasts' demands began to make sense. Even I had had enough of his frolicking speeches.

"Listen," I said bluntly. "How'd you like to get out of here?"

The unicorn blinked its large brown eyes. "At last! The voice of reason! It is painful how few virgins there are around this place! Although—" The unicorn looked at me significantly. "I can sniff one out if I have to."

"Never mind that now!" I said, exasperated. "If you want to get away, there's a job you're going to have to do!"

"No need to get rough!" the unicorn exclaimed. "You know, I don't go in for *any* of that kinky stuff."

"No! No! I need you to carry my master away!"

"Your master? Do you mean—" The beast shook its splendid golden horn. "I do not carry shoes."

"Well, then we'll make a litter, and you can drag the shoe!" I paused. I should not let my frustration with this beast's attitude get the better of me. How would my master handle this?

"Indeed," I added. "It should be no problem for a beast as magnificent as you."

The unicorn hesitated. "Well—"

Brax suddenly appeared between us. "How about an enchanted dagger to put on the end of that horn? I tell you, I have accessories to improve even your best mythological features. The dagger's chrome-plated, too!"

"Doom!" Headbasher came crashing down, narrowly missing the demon.

"Easy terms!" Brax called as it leapt back on stage. "A lifetime to pay!" The warrior's huge bulk lumbered after it.

"Oh, for the verdant fields," the unicorn whispered. It turned to regard me solemnly. "Perhaps we could work something out."

I regained the stage to tell my master.

The two demons were circling the Griffin. Nothing much had changed; everyone was still shouting or running or bellowing or bashing.

"I might be able to sell you a weapon," Brax added hot on Snarks's heels, "guaranteed to do away with pesky demons."

"Excellent idea," the Griffin rumbled in response. "And then I could do away with both of you."

"Wait a moment!" Brax cried. "Do not dare for an instant to compare us! I am but a poor salesdemon, trying to eke out an existence during one of the most turbulent and potentially lucrative times in the history of the world."

"Notice," Snarks retorted, "when he describes himself, he does not resort to the word 'honest.' "

"Why don't you come back to the Netherhells and say that, traitor? Just wait until—urk!"

Headbasher connected with Brax's forehead. There was a dull thud.

"Where was I?" the demon said weakly. "Who was I? What was I?" It disappeared in a cloud of sickly yellow smoke.

"Ah." Snarks smiled. "Teamwork."

"Doom," Hendrek replied.

From within his shoe, my master sneezed mightily.

"Enough!" I shouted, seeing my opening. "The great wizard and his entourage must proceed to Vushta!"

"I think not," the Griffin rumbled, emphatically.

"But what of the demon's warning?" I insisted. "The foul creature implied that the Netherhells has a plan that will destroy us all!"

"A mere charade," the Griffin said, "once you consider it in the pure light of reason. We are familiar with demonic sales practices."

The great winged creature turned to the crowd. "Think upon it, my fellow beasts. Better yet, let me ask the wizard a question. One wonders why he has not used the lightning trick again."

The Griffin strolled over to the shoe and raked it gently with its claws.

"It seems to me that you have some weakness, and must hide within this shoe for a reason. Besides which, it restricts your mobility. Maybe we could learn to dodge lightning, and keep you around for a while. I'm sure, given sufficient time, you could see the mythological point of view—"

"Urk!" the Griffin cried suddenly. "Then again, there are always two sides—"

The Griffin collapsed in a heap of feathers and claws. Headbasher had done its hellish work again.

"Doom," Hendrek intoned.

The crowd of mythological beasts roared as one and surged for the stage.

"I think this might be a good moment to leave," I suggested.

"Uh-oh. It's time for Brownie Power!" The little fellow was once again at my side. "Why don't we wish us out of here?"

The Brownie paused expectantly.

"Oh," I said after a moment. "I wish we were out of here."

"That's more like it! We have to observe the conventions you know. Now, how to do it? A distraction of some sort?" The Brownie glanced at my master.

"The very thing!" He leaned close to me and whispered. "A rain of shoes!"

The Brownie began to dance a merry jig.

There was a rumble in the distance. The crowd paused, startled by the noise. The Hippogriff looked up with some trepidation, anticipating lightning.

From high up in the sky fell a single pair of sandals, tied together by their ankle straps. They bounced off the stage with a muted thump.

"Oh dear," the Brownie fretted. "Not quite what I expected. Well, let's not count that as a wish after all, shall we? Remember, I'm still learning."

The crowd once again approached the stage.

"I wonder how Brownies taste?" something cried.

"Yeah!" something else answered. "Waste not, want not!"

"Wait a moment!" the Brownie cried. "Maybe if I did the tango!"

Both my master's arms emerged from the shoe.

"Doom," Hendrek whispered.

I wished I had my stout oak staff. We would not go down without a fight!

Suddenly, the world went dark. I looked aloft. Something very large plummetted from the sky, blotting out the sun.

"No!" the Hippogriff cried. "Not that!"

But it was. Why hadn't I recognized it? It was, I knew, what I had seen before.

NINE

*There comes a time when a wizard must put his
fate totally in the hands of another. This takes
great courage, and great faith in the ability of
others to perform some function that is beyond
you. But there are benefits to this course of action
as well. Should this task reach a successful conclusion, it will show you the worthiness of your
fellow beings, and lead you to trust in the pro-
vidence of the universe. And, of course, should
the task not be successful, there is always someone
else to blame.*

—*THE TEACHINGS OF EBENEZUM,*
VOLUME XXVII

The crowd dispersed rapidly to make way for the
dragon. The giant reptile landed with a resounding
thud.

"Excuse me, my dear," the dragon said. "Not the
most graceful of landings, I'm afraid. Do you have my
hat?" The reptile turned to the crowd, most of which
was cowering around the edges of the clearing.

"Pardon me," the dragon enunciated. "Did I arrive at an inauspicious moment?"

"Pop! Wake up!" the Hippogriff cried. The Griffin snored, still under Headbasher's awesome power.

The blond woman sitting on the dragon's back reached into a satchel in front of her and extracted a large top hat. She handed it to the dragon.

"Thank you," the giant reptile said as it placed the hat atop its head.

I had thought I knew this dragon! Now, I was sure.

"Hubert!" I cried.

"Good heavens!" The dragon blew a smoke ring of surprise. "Could it be a fan?"

" 'Tis Wuntvor!" I called. "You remember—the Western Kingdoms, and that business with the duke?"

Hubert nodded. "I never forget an engagement. You should see my scrapbook on that one."

"You remember Ebenezum, too?" I pointed across the stage. "Well, at the moment, he's inside that shoe."

"Oh, does he do escapes, too? We had a fellow like that on our bill when we played the Palace. Used to get out of locked trunks and iron maidens, that sort of thing. Never a shoe, though. Rather a unique touch." Hubert nodded his head approvingly.

I wondered if I should correct his line of conjecture. Then again, perhaps it was best if we did not discuss my master's malady in too great detail at present. The crowd seemed to be getting over their shock at the dragon's sudden entrance, and were slowly moving closer to both Hubert and the maiden on his back.

"Hello, Wuntie."

My heart stood still in my chest. Only one woman had ever called me Wuntie, and then only in our most intimate moments. Could it be?

It was! Alea waved from her perch atop the dragon.

It was little wonder I hadn't recognized her. She had changed in the weeks we had been apart. No longer was she but a duke's daughter, forced to while away her hours in a drafty keep deep within the Western Kingdoms. Her hair, once straight, was curled, and seemed a lighter shade than I remembered, probably bleached from hours of flying through sunny skies on a dragon's back. She wore a gown of lightest blue, no doubt all the rage in Vushta. Vushta, the city of a thousand forbidden delights, what a magical place! For when Alea had left on a dragon's back a scant two months before, she had been little more than a girl. Now though, in dress, in manner, in bearing, she seemed a woman of experience, an actress who had taken Vushta by storm, and therefore could do whatever she pleased.

Once, she had been fond of me. And she remembered, for she called me Wuntie!

"Indeed!" my master called from deep within his shoe. Apparently, after everyone had ceased to run madly about, he had gotten an opportunity to regain his breath. "So nice of you to drop by and give us an escort, Hubert!"

"Why, yes! Of course! My pleasure!" The dragon leaned close to me with a chuckle. "I can ad-lib with the best of them," he whispered. He turned to the audience, and spoke with the full power of his dragon lungs.

"Ladies and gentlemen—and assorted beasts—in but a moment from now, you are about to witness a feat designed for the crowned heads of the Continent, yet performed for the first time anywhere on this stage before you. Yes, it's Ebenezum and the Amazing Shoe Escape!"

No! No! This was all wrong! I pulled urgently on the dragon's tail.

"Pop! Wake up!" The Hippogriff nudged its sleeping father with equal urgency.

"Excuse me," Hubert intoned. "I must have a brief conversation with the magician's assistant."

I explained, as briefly as possible, that, rather than have Ebenezum escape from the shoe, the five of us, Hendrek, Snarks and the Brownie included, were attempting to escape from here entirely. If not, I concluded, we were in danger of being eaten.

"Ah," the dragon nodded his head knowingly. "A rough audience, huh? Say no more."

Hubert glanced briefly at Alea, then resumed.

"Actually, it is not mere coincidence that brings me here. We were flying through the air, between engagements, when I spied you in the midst of these monsters. I spoke briefly with Alea, and she agreed, that if we but had the time, we would like to drop in and say hello. And, with such a large crowd, there was always the possibility of staging a show. As itinerant theater people, you know, we must earn our bread wherever we can. But, a previous engagement called."

"But I thought you had gone to Vushta!" I cried. "Didn't they care for your act?"

"Oh, on the contrary, we were quite a hit. Especially our novelty numbers!"

"Yes!" Alea rejoined enthusiastically. "You should have seen the reaction to the 'Maiden and the Rings of Fire' routine!"

"That's right!" Hubert continued. "But that was nothing compared to the big finish, when Alea would play my scales! We'll show you our whole act if we have a chance! We were even offered extended contracts in some of Vushta's choicest nightspots. But I did not want the crowd to become overfamiliar with our act. Always leave them wanting more, that's this dragon's motto!

"In short, you can only play in Vushta for so long. We are on a tour of the provinces, playing the smaller halls, and in some cases," the dragon sighed, "the larger barns. Still, that's show business!"

"Yes," Alea added indignantly. "And they cancelled our last show right out from under us!"

"Something about fire laws!" Hubert snorted a puff of smoke. "What can you expect from farmers!"

"Pop! Wake up!" the Hippogriff wailed. "It's time for leadership!" I looked up to see the crowd of monsters considerably closer to the stage.

"Would you please be quiet?" Hubert roared. "How do you expect artists to prepare?" The dragon raised his snout and sent a column of fire into the air. The crowd decided that some distance was a good idea after all.

"Fine," Hubert puffed contentedly. "Now we must come up with an escape worthy of my talents."

"Couldn't we just run away?" I suggested.

"No, I'm sorry, that just doesn't have the right —*dramatic unity*! I have an image, you know. My fans expect a certain special flare in all my actions. Now that I'm on the verge of becoming one of the true stars of the Vushta stage, it's the least I can do."

"What?" I cried, exasperated. This was all too much! "Do you want our escape accompanied by music?"

"What a wonderful idea!" Hubert blew three perfect smoke rings. "A big song and dance, with Damsel and Dragon, those two toe-tappers all Vushta is talking about, in the foreground, of course. And then we escape! What a finale!"

"Hey, this is the perfect diversion! Talk about Brownie Power!"

I glanced at the little fellow. Now what was he talking about?

"Those sandals that fell from the sky, I just had the

steps wrong! I knew I should have done the tango all along!''

"Oh," Hubert remarked. "A Brownie."

"At last!" the Brownie cried. "A true creature of the world! A fellow who knows quality when he sees it. You'd be surprised, my good dragon, how often we wee folk are confused with Fairies!"

" 'Tis the confusion of the uninformed," the dragon chortled. "You're much too lively to be a Fairy. It's a shame. If Brownies weren't so short, they could have a real future on the stage."

"Short?" The little fellow stamped his tiny feet. "Brownie stereotyping! I'll have you know Brownies are the perfect height! The rest of you creatures are far too tall!"

The Griffin groaned.

"Pop?" the Hippogriff asked hopefully.

"Perhaps we should get under way," I urged.

"Just what should we do?" the dragon asked in a low voice. "As I recall, when I get too close to your master, he begins to sneeze."

"That was before Brownie magic came along—"

"Yes," I cut the little fellow off short, "that shoe somehow protects him from sorcerous influences."

"Excellent!" the dragon cried. "That means the wizard can stay and catch our act!" Hubert tipped his top hat towards the shoe, then turned back to me. "How's this for a plan? At a prearranged signal, the damsel and I will cause a distraction upon the stage. The rest of you will bolt for the forest during the confusion. I'll shoot a little flame around to liven things up a bit more, then join you presently in the forest."

I mentioned that there was only one problem with Hubert's plan. The wizard, trapped in a shoe, was unable to run.

"A small problem, at best," Hubert rejoined. "As long as Ebenezum is in his protective shoe, I should be able to scoop him up and carry him at the end of our performance."

It sounded as if it actually might work. I quickly introduced the dragon to the others in our party.

"Doom," Hendrek remarked.

"A dragon with a top hat?" Snarks peered up at Hubert. "Tell me, why do you feel you need these affectations? Some trouble at home?"

Hubert looked at Snarks with some disdain. "You want me to rescue this?"

"You know," Snarks added, "if you stood up straighter, you'd be much more fearsome. Nobody's really scared of a dragon who slouches."

"Did you see the pretty birdy?" the Griffin intoned. "I saw the pretty birdy!"

"What is this?" Hubert remarked.

"The leader of the group here," I replied, "still somewhat undone by a bash on the head from Hendrek's magic warclub."

"Pop!" the Hippogriff cried. "Pull yourself together! I know I haven't always been the perfect son—"

The Griffin blinked. "Does the birdy have any gold?"

"Wuntvor!" Ebenezum hissed from within his shoe. "I fear the beast is regaining its senses!"

The Griffin staggered to the front of the stage. "Fellow creatures!" It stopped and shook its head. "Ladies, gentlemen, and birdies!" It paused and blinked again.

"Pop! You can do it! I tell you what! No more old-age jokes! That's a promise!"

"Old age?" The Griffin came to its senses with a

roar. "Whosoever has done this to me will feel the wrath of—urk!"

"Thank you, Hendrek," my master remarked.

"Doom," the warrior replied.

There were shouts out in the crowd. They began to move closer to the stage again. If they had started out as a rough audience, I feared they would soon get far rougher.

The dragon cleared his throat. Small flames lapped around his teeth.

"Listen, creatures," he said. "Let's get something straight here. I am a dragon."

"Sure, you can talk!" something shouted. "You've already got *your* maiden!"

"Yeah!" came another voice. "I wonder how she'd taste with salt?"

The dragon roared, sending a shaft of fire thirty feet into the air.

It seemed to quiet the conversationalists in the crowd.

"As I was saying," Hubert continued, "I am the dragon. You are not the dragon. Are there any questions?"

"Yeah!" something replied. "You are the dragon, but you are only one dragon. We here at AFTAO-MAIBAC are many!"

"You here at what?" the dragon said. "Oh, never mind. Look here, fellows, do we really want bloodshed, sizzled flesh, the whole rotten mess? Or would we rather see a show?"

"A show?" the Hippogriff asked.

"Yes!" the dragon cried. "The music, the lights, the laughter! Not only will you see Ebenezum and the amazing shoe trick! As an introduction, you will get to see one of the premier song-and-dance duos of all time!"

"A show?" the Hippogriff repeated.

"Yes!" the dragon reiterated. "For what is a gathering of this size without entertainment? Now, if you will but give us a mere moment to prepare—"

Hubert let the words hang in the air as he turned to our party.

"The element of surprise is on our side, but we will still have to make this quick. We'll do a couple of songs, a little patter, something to put the crowd at their ease. Then, when we get into our big finish, 'Flames of Love,' you folks will have to make a run for it!"

"Flames of love?" Snarks interjected.

"Yes," the dragon nodded. "It is rather poetic, isn't it? So, when the damsel here cries 'Burn me dragon, with the fire of desire,' that's when you should make your exit." The dragon blew a contemplative smoke ring. "It's a shame you won't be able to stick around and see it. Talk about great theater!"

I assured Hubert that we would be glad to witness his performance in its entirety at some other time. Behind us, though, the crowd was busy getting restless again.

"Okay!" Hubert said. "It's time for the big build-up. Are you ready, damsel?"

"Ready, dragon!" Alea called.

"Good enough! Showtime in three minutes!"

The dragon strode out to center stage, careful not to tread on the sleeping Griffin.

Hubert breathed a sheet of flame over the heads of the audience. "And now, to begin the entertainment! A smoke ring demonstration!"

I leaned close to Alea. "What's Hubert doing?"

"Oh, don't mind him." Alea put a reassuring hand on my shoulder. "He's just warming up the crowd."

I felt a little warm myself. I had forgotten what it was like to have someone as wonderful as Alea so close by my side. And she was no longer the girl of the forest whom I had known. Now, she was a woman of Vushta!

I looked deep into her eyes. "Tell me about Vushta," I whispered.

"Vushta?" She laughed, the sound of dew falling on a summer's eve. "Why, it is a magical place, but treacherous as well. One must be careful, or a maiden's honor, yea her very life, may be forfeit!"

"Yes, Alea?" I said, entranced. I wanted to hear it all!

Her blue eyes looked deep into my own. "Yes, Wuntie, Vushta is almost like a different world. It makes one think about where one has been, and sometimes—" Her hand moved down my shoulder, running gently along my arm. "Sometimes it makes one realize how much one misses what one has left behind."

I swallowed. "Yes, Alea?"

"Yes, Wuntvor, when you are an actress on the Vushta stage, whole new worlds open up to you. Many men would like to court you; worldly men, versed in magic and every other art. But, with their worldly ways comes a cynicism, a shell they keep around themselves so they cannot truly touch others, or be touched in return." Her nails stroked my knuckles just before her fingers intertwined with mine. "Wuntie, it makes one long for a simple, homespun boy like you."

"Yes, Alea," I whispered, barely able to get the words out. My throat had suddenly become very dry. It had something to do with how warm the world had become in the last few minutes. A late summer heat spell, perhaps, or the warm spring glow that came from Alea's eyes.

She turned toward the stage for an instant, her blond curls shining in the sun. Hubert was stomping back and forth on the worn floorboards, breathing rings of fire. The crowd seemed uncertain how to respond. Isolated cheers came when Hubert breathed a fire pretzel. However, I thought I heard low grumbling out there as well.

I looked back at the woman who once had been mine. Simple? Homespun? Alea's words began to sink into my overheated consciousness. How strange were the fates! When we had first known each other, back in Wizard's Woods, she had wanted me for my worldliness. Now, she wanted me because I reminded her of home.

Alea turned back to me, her eyes full of excitement, and kissed me full on the lips.

"Do I look all right?" she asked brightly. "Everything in place? It's almost time for my entrance!"

I was having some difficulty breathing. "Yes, Alea," I managed at last.

She stood up. "Okay, Hubert!" she spoke in a hoarse whisper. "Let's break a wing!"

I shook my head in an attempt to clear it. Alea's attentions were all very nice, but somehow, all wrong. There was someone else.

"Norei!" I cried aloud.

I swallowed hard. I realized then that I must stop thinking thoughts of Alea. I was promised to another!

The audience was getting rougher. Cries of "AFTAOMAIBAC!" and "Let's fire the dragon!" wafted my way.

Hubert paused in his demonstration. "All right, fellow creatures!" he called out. "You want change?"

A ragged cheer rose from the crowd.

"You want excitement?" the dragon cried.

The answering cheer was stronger this time.

"Then how about this? Take it, damsel!"

Alea ran up to the dragon's side. They broke into song:

We do the dragon walk, from town to town.
We do the dragon walk, we really get around.
When we go steppin', people get kinda shy,
'Cause when you're stepped on by a dragon, good-
*   bye!*

Alea proceeded to perform an elaborate tap dance between the dragon's toes. Hubert hummed to give her musical accompaniment.

"Doom!" Hendrek said. "So now we prepare ourselves." He nervously shifted his grip on Head-basher as he watched the audience through half-closed eyes. "This plan strikes me as difficult, at best."

Snarks nodded his head in agreement. "I never knew I would end like this, a victim of musical comedy."

"Come on, guys!" a small voice piped. "Don't be so glum! You've got a Brownie on your side!" The Brownie did a little dance in time with Hubert's humming. "There's more than a dragon here to depend on. I've got another wish or two up my sleeve, let me tell you!"

"Wuntvor?" my master's voice called from his shoe. "Exactly what is happening?"

I realized then that my master, in his shoe, sitting on the far side of the stage, would have been unable to hear our whispers and thus knew nothing of our plan. I ran quickly to his side. Too quickly, for I did not watch my feet.

I tripped over the Griffin.

"What? Where?" the beast mumbled, still half-asleep. "Look at the two birdies!"

I explained the situation as briefly as I could.

"Indeed," Ebenezum replied. "You show great in-itiative, Wuntvor. Should you grow out of your clum-siness, you will make a great wizard." My master again poked his hands into the outside air. "I have managed to recover quite a bit. This shoe, silly looking as it is, offers a great deal of protection. Alas, we have learned that the protection is not total, but it should be more than enough to suit our purposes."

Ebenezum waved his hands about. There was the sound of distant thunder. "Yes," the wizard said. "Quite fully recovered. While the dragon's plan might have been somewhat problematic with me in my sneezing state, I can now lend a hand with a well-placed spell or two. We should be on our way to Vushta in no time."

I ran back to the others. I felt as though I might leap with joy! With Ebenezum once again able to perform magic, we could not fail!

"Hello, birdy," the Griffin mumbled as I passed. "Yummy, yummy birdy."

Still, I reflected as I reached the others, the sooner we were out of here, the better I would feel.

The assembled beasts seemed to have stopped shouting. I glanced at Damsel and Dragon's performance. If they had not quieted the crowd, at least they had them reasonably stunned. Hubert had now taken center stage, and was singing a sensitive ballad.

> *My flame's gone out,*
> *I don't feel bold.*
> *My legs don't work,*
> *And my wings don't fold.*
> *When I sun myself*
> *My blood's still cold.*
> *I'm just a lizard in love.*

Snarks sidled over to me. He jabbed a thumb at the singing dragon. "Couldn't we escape a few minutes early?"

"No, no," I whispered back. "Everything is set. The wizard even has a spell or two up his sleeve."

"Doom," Hendrek said, a hopeful note in his voice.

"Wow!" a small voice piped. "A dragon, a wizard, and a Brownie! Talk about your triple threats!"

The Griffin raised its head.

"Birdies. Birdies everywhere."

I turned toward Hubert and Alea, silently hoping they would speed up their act. I did not wish to end up as a birdy.

Alea finished a song about being just a maiden in a dragon tower that seemed to remind some members of the audience why they were here in the first place. She and Hubert ignored the shouts and began their snappy patter.

"Get ready!" I whispered to the others. "It's going to come at any time now!"

"Say, dragon?"

"Yes, damsel?"

"How do you pick up lady dragons?"

Hubert breathed a ball of flame. "I say 'Hey, baby, want to have a hot time?' "

Alea and Hubert began a dance number.

"I knew there was a catch to this plan!" Snarks muttered. "In order to hear the escape line, we have to listen to their act!"

I looked sharply at the demon. We had to suffer through this together. The rest of our party listened in grim silence.

"Help! I'm a damsel in distress!"

"Really? I didn't know!"

"Oh, sure! But as soon as the show is over, I'm going back stage to change into dat dress!"

Their dance number grew faster.

"Maybe we should let the monsters eat us," Snarks suggested. "It would be a kinder end."

"Birdies." The Griffin was on its feet. "Pretty, pretty birdies." The beast staggered toward us.

"Doom!" Hendrek raised Headbasher aloft once again.

"Oh, no, you don't!" The Hippogriff reared up before us. "You've bopped my pop once too often! Make one more move, you get a hoof in the head!"

"Birdies." The Griffin made smacking sounds with its beak. "Yummy, yummy, pretty birdies."

"But what if he eats one of us?" I pointed out.

The Hippogriff shook its head. "That's the least you should let him do after the way you've treated him. What kind of guests are you, anyway?"

I felt the floorboard shake ever so slightly by my feet. The Brownie was doing a dance. Hendrek grumbled deep in his throat, both hands on Headbasher. And both my master's arms were free of the shoe, ready to conjure.

"Are we hot, damsel?"

"We're hot, dragon, and we're getting hotter!"

The audience did not seem to agree. I heard a dozen angry shouts. The crowd began to surge forward.

"But we can get hotter, can't we, damsel?"

"Yes, we can make it hot! So hot!"

This must be the build-up to their last big number. The signal to escape was coming at last!

"Yummy birdy." I felt something grab my shirt. I looked down, and saw that I was held by a Griffin claw.

"Tell me, damsel!" Hubert screamed. "How hot do you want it?"

"Burn me, dragon, with the fire—" Alea's voice died away as she watched a huge bird descend from the sky.

"Hey! Cool it! Stop everything!" the great bird cried. It landed on the edge of the stage, in front of the dragon.

The crowd paused in its surge. Hubert stopped his patter. Everyone froze where they stood, eyes on the Rok.

"Man, you know I don't shake easy." The Rok pointed its beak to the sky. "But just feast your eyes on that!"

My mouth opened when I looked up. Now we were in real trouble!

TEN

It is of tremendous importance, when a wizard enters a battle, that he should have prepared sufficient spells beforehand to meet anything he might face during the coming fight. It is even more important that the wizard act bravely during the course of the fight, so that he might do credit to the names of wizards everywhere. And what happens should the magician's army lose the fray? Of the greatest importance of all, therefore, is the wizard's insistence that, before the battle, he be paid in full.

— *THE TEACHINGS OF EBENEZUM,*
VOLUME III

"Look at all the pretty birdies!"

The Griffin's claw dropped from my shirt as it turned to stare.

Hundreds of dark shapes filled the sky.

" 'Tis the Netherhells!" I heard Ebenezum shout.

"Doom!" Hendrek cried.

Was this, then, the Forxnagel? Was everything we

had worked on for so long truly over? Would I never see Vushta, city of a thousand forbidden delights?

Alea ran across the stage and threw herself into my arms. She kissed me passionately.

"If this is the end, Wuntie," she breathed in my ear, "I want to die held by a simple, country boy."

The warmth of her kiss almost made me forget what I had seen. But the sight had been too chilling for even Alea's passion to erase. I turned away from the woman to look at the sky again.

They were closer now, hundreds upon hundreds of demons with wings. At a distance, I thought many of them seemed to have two heads, but I saw now that some of the winged creatures held two-footed demon riders. Then again, others in that flying congregation did have two heads. It was a truly fearsome sight.

"Wuntvor!" my master called. "Gather our party together! We face great odds, but we are not without our resources. We must fight them together!"

I turned to the others. "Hendrek! Hubert! Snarks! Brownie! We rally around the shoe!"

There was a sharp banging behind me. I turned to see the unicorn, beating its golden horn on the edge of the stage.

"Wait a moment!" the splendid beast cried. "I am not with these creatures! I thought we had a bargain!"

In the heat of events, I had completely forgotten the silly creature. The heavens knew we could use all the help we could get. Still, would a beast that spent all its time standing around looking fantastically beautiful really be all that handy?

"Um," I answered indecisively. "What would you like to do?"

"Why, fight magnificently for freedom, of course."

The unicorn snorted and pawed the soft earth. "I have been imprisoned. If I escaped, they would only bring me back here again. Now, though, I see a chance to roam the verdant hills again. How much better your party will fight, with a noble unicorn to guide them on!"

The beast reared upon its hind legs. "Unicorns also make a very attractive centerpiece if you're contemplating painting the scene of battle." It raised its golden horn toward the sun. "See?"

"Wuntvor!" my master called.

The demons were almost upon us!

"Pop!" the Hippogriff cried nervously.

"What?" The Griffin shook itself and blinked. "Those aren't birdies. Those are demons! What is going on here?"

A voice called down from on high:

> "Guxx and his demons have come today,
> And soon will hold the world in sway!"

"Join us, then!" I called to the unicorn. " 'Tis the dread, rhyming demon, Guxx Unfufadoo!" We would need all the help we could get to defeat this fiend quickly, for, with every rhyme the demon made, its power grew!

The unicorn leapt upon the stage with a movement so graceful that it took my breath away.

The great beast's nostrils flared. "Then let them fight a unicorn!"

"Wait a second here!" the Griffin shouted to the sky. "Do you have an invitation?"

The demons appeared to be tightening into battle formation.

"Doom!" Hendrek was at my side. "Come. We will

form a circle around the shoe. That way we can defend ourselves, until Hubert and the wizard find an opening."

So Ebenezum was well enough to guide us into battle. Somehow, despite the hopeless odds, I began to think we might see Vushta after all.

But oh, for my stout oak staff! I looked over at the corner of the stage where the Griffin had done much of its wood shredding. Well, if I had no staff, a plank would have to do. I quickly found a loose board of sufficient size.

Alea was waiting for me in the battle circle. "Oh, Wuntie," she cried. "Our last moments—together!"

I wished she wouldn't kiss me that way. It disturbed my concentration. Still, if you were going to your death, I imagined there was worse preparation.

"You'll be able to fight better if you start breathing again," Snarks suggested. "And you'd probably get better leverage if you held that board a little lower. Well, I don't need to mention your posture again, but you could have a more efficient stance if you—"

"You shouldn't be doing this!" the Griffin bellowed aloft, causing Snarks to pause midsentence. "We have an agreement with the Netherhells!"

The rider on the first flying demon replied:

"Your claims to my ears sound absurd,
For soon demons will rule the world."

"It is Guxx all right," I muttered. The talent behind that particular poem wiped all doubt from my mind.

Snarks nodded grimly. "For rhymes that bad, his power should decrease."

The unicorn snorted, and looked at me with its large,

soulful eyes. "I would probably be much more effective if I had a rider."

I hefted my new-found plank experimentally. "A rider?" I asked.

"Yes!" the unicorn replied with half-closed eyes. "Someone to ride with me, nobly into battle." The beast sighed. "I tell you, it's been so long since I've had a virgin by my side."

"Oh, Wuntvor!" Alea whispered. "Look at the creature! How beautiful!"

I breathed a sigh of relief. Apparently, Alea had not quite caught what the beautiful beast implied. But Alea! Now that was an idea! I turned back to the unicorn. "Why not let the woman ride you?"

The unicorn glanced briefly at Alea. "Sorry. Not interested." The beast lowered its horn. "Oh, but my head is so heavy! Oh, for a virgin lap before battle!"

I decided this might be a good time to confer with Ebenezum on battle strategy.

"All right," the Griffin was saying a little uncertainly. "Well, perhaps you weren't invited. But there's always room for a few more. Why don't you just land your troops in that field over there, and we mythological beasts can get on with our meeting. You wouldn't happen to have brought any gold? No, no, silly of me to assume— Well, we're all friends here. Why don't you land? We'll even let you bring up points of business."

Guxx pointed at the shoe.

> *"You harbor my enemy!*
> *You are no friend of me!"*

The rhymes were getting worse. I began to wish the demons would attack.

I looked up at Guxx. He was close enough now so that I could make out what would, for want of better words, be called facial features. If anything, the demon was more hideous than I remembered. His skin was still a sickly, dark green, and his evil smile betrayed a mouth that was far too wide, with far too many teeth. Now, though, the demon sported something new—a mane of what looked like bright red hair.

" 'Tis much worse than I thought!" Snarks shuddered. "Guxx has made himself the Grand Hoohah!"

"The Grand Hoohah?" I asked, taken aback. "What is the Grand Hoohah?"

Snarks turned to me, his face a mixture of fear and pity. "Trust me!" he whispered. "You don't want to know!"

My eyes slid from Guxx, who was shouting order poems to his lieutenants, to the demon beast that he rode. I wished I hadn't looked. The thing was the color of yellow clay after a rainstorm, except for its eyes, which seemed to glow green from within. It had the requisite fangs and claws that seemed to be standard equipment for all creatures of the Netherhells. It nodded at me and licked its lips.

"Dinner," it said.

Moments before, I had anticipated being eaten by some of the less ethical members of the mythological community. Somehow, that now appeared greatly preferable to the option currently before me.

"Much worse," Snarks muttered. "The Grand Hoohah? Much worse. Oh, why did I have to leave the Netherhells? Oh, why did I have to turn honest?" The demon nervously chewed upon his stubby fingers.

For an instant, the world was still. I knew then that the battle was about to begin.

"Boy!" The Brownie began to dance furiously. "Is it time for Brownie Power!"

"For a change," Snarks whispered, "I wish the Brownie was right. What can he do? Give everybody a hot foot?"

"Why don't you go suggest it?" I asked.

But there was no time. Guxx lifted both his demonic arms and mussed up his flaming red badge of office. A hundred hideous things began their descent from the sky.

Guxx screamed:

"Now our foes will get their due!
Minutes from now we'll have wizard stew!"

"Wait a second!" the Griffin was shouting. "You know that mythological beasts should be strictly neutral in arguments of this sort! What about the Camelot Convention?"

"Drive our enemies to the ground!
First demonic horde, go down!"

The wizard's hands shot up in the air. I could hear my master's muffled voice shout a quick string of mystic words.

The first group of demons plummetted toward earth.

Until they suddenly slowed down, then stopped, then started plummetting up. Their alarmed cries faded into the upper air.

"Simple gravity reversal spell," my master explained. He sneezed once. "Pardon me," he intoned. His hands disappeared within the shoe to seek out his handkerchief.

"Think twice about what you are doing here!" the Griffin called upward. "If you want us to get out of your way, just let us know. Don't be hasty! Remember the Mabinogion Accord!"

Guxx roared at his first setback. He tore furiously at his red headdress:

"Now it's time we start to fight,
Second demon horde, take flight!"

Ebenezum was still busy blowing his nose!

"Hubert!" I called. "It's up to you!"

"A command performance!" the dragon yelled back. He took a deep breath and shot out a ball of flame half his size. The second horde dispersed in panic. The fire-ball consumed all but the quickest. The few survivors fell fighting among the crowd.

"Hold it a second here!" the Griffin called. "Now, if we all keep cool heads, we can avoid bloodshed! We're really just one big happy family after all, aren't we? Remember the Grendel Non-Aggression Pact?"

Guxx was enraged. Handfuls of his red crown fell to earth.

"Attack, third horde! Give them a lickin'!
Don't forget their leader with the head of a
*   chicken!"*

"What?" the Griffin roared. "AFTAOMAIBAC! Let's wipe these vermin from the face of the earth!"

The Griffin took flight, followed by the Rok and the Hippogriff. The dragon took another deep breath.

"Stay, friend Hubert!" Ebenezum called. "Now that there are other than demons on the field of battle, we will have to be more selective in our attack."

"Well, if you say so," Hubert said reluctantly. "They weren't a very good audience."

"Make way! Make way!" cried a small voice, barely audible in the melee. "It's Brownie time!"

There was a crash of thunder twice as loud as anything Ebenezum had produced.

Cries of alarm came from the demons overhead, followed by a great banging, as if someone were beating upon the Netherhells horde with drumsticks.

"Cover your heads! Cover your heads! In a moment, we'll be getting the fallout." The Brownie laughed delightedly. "I knew I should have used the tango!"

Shoes fell everywhere. Boots, slippers, sandals, those funny things with the curved toes that you found in the Eastern Kingdoms; if it could be called a shoe, it fell. So did demons. Hundreds of them scattered on the stage and through the crowd.

Now the battle began in earnest.

I moved close by my master's shoe, my new-found plank held high. The wizard Ebenezum was the key to this battle. I would protect his shoe to my last ounce of strength, so that he might concentrate upon his spells. Come, demons, I thought! But for some reason, the fiends of the Netherhells were keeping their distance.

I looked around to see my compatriots in the midst of the fray. Headbasher whirled about Hendrek's head, leading the immense man in a complex dance, thrashing and clubbing his way through the throng. Hendrek moved in an entirely different way when he held his weapon, leaping and pirouetting with a grace that seemed highly improbable in one of his bulk. It was almost as if the enchanted club controlled the warrior, not the other way around. Cries of "Doom!" and "Urk!" filled the air.

Snarks had managed to find a staff of some sort, and

was playing a complicated game with a whole force from the Netherhells. The truth-telling demon would shout something out to one of his opponents that seemed to outrage the Netherhells denizen so that it would rush at Snarks in a blind anger. Snarks would then render the demon foe unconscious with a sharp rap from his staff, and confront the next enemy in line.

Why weren't they attacking my master? For a second, I felt as if I should leave the wizard's side and wade out into the midst of things, dealing destruction with my sturdy plank. But perhaps the demons were not attacking for fear of the combined might of a wizard's magic and an apprentice's muscle. Maybe they wished to distract me, and attack Ebenezum when his guard was gone.

My master's hands once again emerged from their protective shoe. Now we would show them a thing or two! His hands made a complex series of mystic passes in the air. A close-packed group of demons howled hideously as they began to sink into the earth, accompanied by a loud sucking sound. Soon, they had disappeared altogether, leaving nothing but a muddy expanse of ground. There was a final loud rumble, as if some underground gases had escaped from a hidden fissure. That corner of the battleground fell silent.

"Simple mud activation spell," Ebenezum remarked. This time, though, he sneezed deeply a half-dozen times.

A great deal of noise still came from overhead. I looked up to see the Griffin, the Hippogriff and the Rok surrounding the still-airborne Guxx.

"I'll teach you not to bring any gold!" the Griffin shouted.

"Careful, Pop!" the Hippogriff warned. "He's a

magic demon, after all. We need to employ some strategy!"

"I can dig it," the Rok remarked. "Why don't you two cats grab his arms while I rip off his head?"

Guxx tossed handfuls of red hair at his attackers.

"Rip his head, they say with glee
Fourth demon horde, attack these three!"

A horrible cry arose as a hundred more demons came screaming through a bank of clouds. Rok, Griffin and Hippogriff flew in different directions.

"There're too many of them!" screamed a panicked mythological creature. "We'll never defeat them!"

"On the contrary," a deep voice rumbled. "They have already lost the battle."

A dozen creatures turned to face the large gray shape.

"What do you mean?" one of them said.

"Simple," the gray shape replied. "They have never faced wombling!"

With that, the Bog Wombler began to roll and shake simultaneously. The demons in the vicinity didn't have a chance.

But there was a host of demons above us as well! Hubert lessened their numbers with well-placed spears of flame, while Alea held tight to the dragon's tail.

"Now!" she cried.

The tail crashed down on three demons who had wandered too close.

"What an act!" Alea cried as she examined the squashed remains. "If only the critics could see us now!"

"It takes two to tango!" a small voice cried.

"I've got you!" a demon yelled as it leapt for the

Brownie. "Mzzmflx! Grzzllbllg!" The demon fell from the stage, its mouth full of shoes.

The unicorn leapt upon the stage, impaling demons upon its razor-sharp horn, then tossing them jauntily aside with but a flick of its well-muscled neck. The gorgeously sweating beast paused before me.

"Ride with me!" the unicorn cried. "How magnificent I look destroying demons. How attractive their blood appears, set off by my shining, golden horn."

The beautiful beast sighed, a single tear forming in one dark eye. "Yet I am incomplete. Oh, with the proper rider, how even more magnificent I would be!"

I mentioned that I was certain it had a point, but this was not the best time to discuss it.

"Wuntvor?"

Thankfully, my master interrupted.

The wizard blew his nose. "If you would move a bit? I need a better view aloft."

As I hastily scrambled to the side of the shoe, Ebenezum's hands once again emerged. Magic words and motions came in quick succession.

The cloud the demons had passed through grew hands. Dozens of hands. They began slapping any demons near enough to reach. Confusion reigned in the sky.

The wizard blew his nose again. "That should give our side a little time."

"I thought we would lose the battle for sure," I admitted.

"Indeed. Yet I was prepared. Demon hordes always come in fours. 'Twas nothing more than a simple cloud-hand formation—"

Suddenly, the wizard began to sneeze as though the shoe weren't even there.

The wizard gasped for air. "I've done too much . . . need to rest . . . keep the others away, for but a moment." The sneezing resumed.

My master had overextended himself! Well, I had stayed by his side in case he needed me. Now, I was his sole protection. I gripped my plank with a new ferocity.

I heard a great scream overhead. Despite the rain of shoes and slapping hands, Guxx had somehow managed to stay aloft. He stared at my master's shoe with naked hatred.

"The wizard spoils my every plan!
But now I'll go end his lifespan!"

That was why no one had attacked. The other demons had saved the shoe for Guxx! He would have to get through me before he could assault my master! I would beat away the demon Guxx with my plank!

Guxx landed on the stage with a mighty thump. I found myself face to face with Guxx's demon mount.

"Dinner."

"Eat wood, foul fiend!" I cried, swinging my plank.

To my surprise, the demon took a large bite out of my plank with razor teeth. It chewed thoughtfully. "Not bad," it remarked, "but I much prefer human flesh."

"Indeed." Ebenezum blew his nose behind me. "Haven't we met somewhere before?"

The demon Guxx ripped off his red headdress and threw it on the floor before the wizard.

"You've forgotten Guxx, you wizard upstart,
But you'll remember me when I tear you apart!"

"Let me think," Ebenezum replied. "I do feel that I

know you from somewhere. One meets so many demons, you know, that they all run together after a while."

Guxx screamed:

> *"I'm one demon you can't mistake,*
> *For I'll have your head upon a plate!"*

"Indeed," Ebenezum remarked. "For a while, I thought you were attempting poetry. I used to know a demon who always attempted poetry. Unpleasant fellow. Never bathed, either. Luckily though, you don't seem to be saying anything that could even be considered a rhyme."

Guxx jumped up and down and shook his fists.

> *"I'll teach you to mock my poetry!*
> *Now Guxx will go and kill his foe—et—*
> *Er, that doesn't work."*

The demon cleared his throat.

> *"So you criticize my poems!*
> *But soon you'll be nothing but broken bo—"*

The demon stomped his clawed foot in frustration.

"Your pardon," the wizard said. "If you'll excuse me for a moment while I free my hands?"

"Enough of this little drama!" The demon mount facing me swallowed the remains of my plank in a single gulp. "We have our own destinies to decide. And yours, good fellow, rests within my stomach. Glmmphmtt zzzznrrbbtt!"

The demon's mouth was full of shoes.

"Brownie Power to the rescue!" a small voice piped.

The demon mount swallowed all the shoes in one gulp. "Trying to fill me up won't do. Flying is hard work. Airborne demons are insatiable!" It paused in its pursuit for an instant to look down. "And Brownies make an excellent dessert!"

"No, you don't!" a magnificently modulated voice cried. "A unicorn will save you!"

The flying demon belched. "It's much too crowded and noisy down here. Wreaks havoc on one's digestion." The creature flew straight up in the air, barely missing a death blow from a golden horn as the unicorn came galloping across the stage.

My master had begun another series of mystic passes. Guxx, momentarily preoccupied with determining a proper rhyme, screamed in anger.

> *"No more spells, don't even start,*
> *For now I'll tear your shoe apart!"*

Guxx launched himself straight for the wizard. The shoe rocked with the force of his landing as Guxx grabbed both of my master's gesticulating hands. The air was filled with shouts of both demon and wizard, Ebenezum attempting desperately to complete a spell, Guxx madly trying to devise poems to increase his power.

The flying demon had settled back upon the stage. "There, now that the horse with the horn is gone. I hate to eat and run, but sometimes—urk!"

"Doom. Headbasher does its hellish work again."

Hendrek turned toward the furiously struggling Guxx and Ebenezum. The giant shoe seemed to be leaping across the stage of its own accord.

"Demon!" I heard Ebenezum gasp. "If you do not release me . . . there will be . . . "

"Stop your threats, my enemy!" Guxx replied. "For I shall soon rend—uh—thee. No, that doesn't work, either!"

My master's criticism had totally undermined the demon's poetic confidence. Perhaps this battle could be won!

My master gasped again. ". . . trouble."

Ebenezum then sneezed one of the world's great sneezes.

The shoe exploded outward, taking Guxx with it to some distant place. Only Hendrek's intervening bulk saved me from being blown off the stage. Even the mighty warrior, thick and heavy as he was, staggered back from the ferocity of the blast.

The warrior's great size blocked my view of the rest of the stage. What had happened to my master?

Hendrek turned to me.

"Doom," he said.

ELEVEN

Perhaps I have given you the wrong impression. A wizard's life is not all fame, fortune and frivolity. There must be periods of rest as well, when a wizard should find a safe retreat where he can seclude himself from sorcery and restore his health and vitality in the proper ascetic atmosphere. While lengthy retreats can deplete a wizard's fortunes, I have always preferred the ascetic atmosphere present in the pleasure gardens of Vushta, where a dozen handmaidens can attend to your every need. And the budget-conscious sorcerer should be sure to ask about their special midweek retreat package plans.

—THE TEACHINGS OF EBENEZUM,
VOLUME XCV (SPECIAL ANNUAL SUPPLEMENT)

"Demons are no match for mythology!"

The Griffin landed on the edge of what was left of the stage. "Let us crush our few remaining foes! Shout out our victory! AFTAOMAIBAC! AFTAOMAIBAC! AFTAOMAIBAC!"

The cheers grew stronger as the remaining demons took hasty flight or were soundly thrashed.

I quickly stepped to Hendrek's side, and looked to where my master had sat within his shoe. There was nothing left but a gaping hole.

I felt a sudden chill. Had the great sneeze exploded not only the shoe, but Ebenezum as well?

Something sneezed beneath my feet.

Joy buoyed my sinking heart. My master had managed to sneeze himself into the crawl space beneath the stage!

"Master!" I cried, and was rewarded with a muffled "Indeed."

A moment's pause, and the wizard spoke again. "Wuntvor? If you might assist me for an instant?"

I clambered into the hole. It was dark down here after the brilliant sunshine above. I blinked in an attempt to orient myself.

My master's sneeze told me the way.

Dim light filtered through from where the Griffin had torn up a corner of the stage. I crawled a few feet to find the wizard tangled in a mass of robes and leather.

I asked my master if he had hurt anything.

"Nothing but what few shreds of dignity I had remaining," the wizard replied. "But there is no time for dignity now. There is only time for Vushta."

The wizard shifted and groaned. "Now, Wuntvor, if you might help disentangle me?" He grunted as I pulled away the bottom of the shoe. "Thank the stars for that cushioned insole. If the shoe had not been so well made, I might have been more seriously hurt."

Ebenezum withdrew his arm as I tried to disengage cloth from leather. His sorcerous robes appeared to be more shredded than before.

"Five demon hordes!" Ebenezum shook his head.

"Not four, but five! Trust the Netherhells to devise fiendish innovations." He replaced his arm in what remained of his sleeve. "How fares the battle above?"

I told him that it was all but done, with the beasts dealing with a remaining demon here and there.

"We have been fortunate there," the wizard agreed. "As powerful as Guxx is, it appears that his strategy is as poor as his poetry."

The wizard was free at last. Ebenezum stretched and sneezed.

"We must be away from here, and hurriedly. Beneath the stage, I am somewhat protected, but once I reach the open air, my malady will return full force." The wizard chewed on his moustache for a moment, considering his options. "Wuntvor, I need you to speak with the dragon. When I emerge, I will need Hubert to carry me immediately out into the forest, while I hold my breath as best I can. Once I am out of range of these mythological creatures, I will have a chance to recover. And that will give you and the rest of the party time to join me on foot, so that we may be on our way to Vushta!"

Vushta! I jumped up to do my master's bidding.

"Wuntvor! Watch your head! It would be best to get to Vushta in one piece."

Rubbing my head where it had smacked the underside of the stage, I crawled back through the hole into sunlight.

"I will call you as soon as things are ready!" I said to my master as I left.

The flying demon that had been Guxx's mount lay on the stage. It must have recovered from Headbasher's blow, for green blood was flowing freely from half a dozen new wounds, including one about the right shape for a unicorn horn. It looked up at me and groaned.

"I guess you won't be my dinner now," it whispered.

"No," I murmured back. "I guess not." There was a roughness in my throat. It was sad to watch even a demon die. "Then Guxx left you behind?"

"Yes," the demon said. "Even after he became Grand Hoohah."

"Grand Hoohah?"

"Don't ask!" the creature gibbered. "You don't want to know!" The demon licked dry lips. "It's not fair! You look so tasty. Just the right fat-to-muscle ratio. Maybe—" The creature winced. "—as a favor to a dying demon—you'd let me nibble a finger or two?"

I stepped hastily away as the thing made one last pitiful attempt to chew.

Hubert was deep in discussion with the Griffin.

"Well, of course!" the Griffin was saying. "No hard feelings! Without your considerable help, we would never have defeated the demons!"

"Pop!" the Hippogriff put in. "If they hadn't been here, we wouldn't have had to fight any demons at all!"

The Griffin turned on the boy. "A fight with a demon is a fight with a demon! What's the matter with you kids today?" The creature turned back to the dragon, shaking its head. "That's the trouble with these youngsters—no perspective. You know, when my son meets strangers, he hardly ever thinks to demand their gold. I mean, we raise them from infants, and this is the thanks we get—"

"Excuse me," I said somewhat timidly. But, as afraid as I was of interrupting this imposing creature, I was even more afraid that the Griffin would never stop talking. "May I have a word with Hubert?"

"What did I tell you?" the Griffin began, but he quieted when the dragon turned to me. I quickly told Hubert of the wizard's request.

"Well," the dragon said reluctantly, "I was hoping

for an encore." He looked wistfully out to the audience, who seemed too preoccupied with dragging away the dead and wounded to be in the mood for light entertainment. "Still, no one has asked. I shall have a short talk with Alea, then I shall be ready. When one thinks of it, it *is* a very dramatic exit."

"We'll be ready in just a moment, master!" I called. As the dragon had moved away, I looked up with some trepidation to see if the Griffin was still annoyed, but the leader of the conference was now in deep discussion with the unicorn.

The beast shook its mane. Long, white hair flared wonderfully in the wind.

"Let bygones be bygones," the unicorn intoned. "These are perilous times, which call for noble and magnificent measures. And who better to suggest such measures than myself?" The beast paused and struck a pose that took my breath away. "The fight with the Netherhells is not yet over. We need to join together to weather this crisis. You have had a fine idea, but it has not been taken far enough! What is needed is a true alliance of all mythical creatures, Griffin and unicorn, Hippogriff and dragon!"

"Maybe," the Griffin replied dubiously. "I'll have to check the bylaws. Might there be any gold in it?"

"What need have we for gold, when a unicorn leads the way?" The grand creature snorted a fine mist from its nostrils. "I will, of course, be first on your new membership list."

"What?" The Griffin flapped its wings furiously. "I'll rip off your horn, you conceited beast! It's probably the only part of you worth anything!"

Alea bounded across the stage and into my arms, causing me to lose interest in the argument.

"Oh, Wuntie!" she breathed. "Hubert tells me he's

going to fly the wizard out of here, and I'm to walk overland with you!" She hugged me tightly. "Oh, it all sounds so adventurous!"

"Yes, Alea," I said through the mass of blond curls that covered my face. I turned my head. "Hendrek! Snarks! Brownie! Get your gear together! We must be off for Vushta!"

The Griffin looked up sharply from listening to the Hippogriff talk about how the unicorn might not have such a bad idea.

"You know, Pop," the Hippogriff said, "that unicorn is really kind of cute. I've been thinking, maybe ocelots are not for me. Give me a chance to get to know that big, beautiful horse a little better—"

"What?" the Griffin cried in my direction. "You can't leave now. We have treaties to sign! Accords to iron out! Amounts of gold must be exchanged!"

Hubert shook his large, befanged dragon head. "No. We must go. There will be other demon attacks. The fate of Vushta, indeed, the fate of the world, depends on us now. Were we to hold back another day, there might be no tomorrow."

"Oh," the Griffin said. "Well, if you put it that way."

I, too, was impressed. Listening to Hubert describe our actions in his stentorian tones made them sound desperately vital. I began to see advantages in having an actor deal with matters of diplomacy.

I knelt at the edge of the hole and exchanged a few words with my master.

"Fellow creatures!" the Griffin spoke to the assemblage. "Our friends must leave, on matters so urgent that all our lives may depend on their actions. We have fought beside them, and, though we have only known them a few hours, have grown to accept them as comrades. We will miss them! We wish them good weather and good speed!''

With that, the wizard emerged from the hole and, holding his nose, sat quickly upon Hubert's back. The dragon gave a brief wave to the crowd. "Until next time!" he cried. "We love you all! Up, up, and away!"

Dragon and rider were soon lost among the clouds.

"You have witnessed Brownie Power today!" a small voice shouted to the audience. "May you be blessed with the luck of the Brownies!"

Snarks added: "And after the two minutes it takes to use that up, I hope you have other luck as well."

"Then again," the Griffin said, "we may not miss all of you."

"Doom!" Hendrek remarked, and we were on our way.

We made our way rapidly through the Enchanted Forest. According to my last-minute conference with the wizard, we were to meet him at the first river crossing of the eastern path. It seemed the best possible landmark in an unfamiliar terrain, but I had no idea how far away that first river might be. So, while I felt it was imperative that we reach Vushta with all speed, I realized that we must pace ourselves at no more than a steady march so that we might have strength for the rest of our journey.

As a result, my compatriots had some opportunity to talk.

"Doom," Hendrek said. "We fight greater and greater battles with the Netherhells. Every fight, I fear, shall be our last. Still, we survive."

"My truth-telling instincts say that there must be a reason for this." Snarks's bright green demon face was set in a ponderous frown. "I knew Guxx before I was banished from the Netherhells. We are vaguely related, you see. He is a fifth cousin on my grandmother's side, and we used to meet at these ceremonies called 'Family Picnics.' Auggh! What ghastly affairs! They gave a new definition to boredom. Be thankful you have not yet devised such tortures here on the surface world!''

"Doom," Hendrek murmured in sympathy.

"So, as I said," Snarks continued, "I am somewhat familiar with Guxx Unfufadoo. He is evil, underhanded, dishonest, cruel, ruthless—in short, perfect leadership material for the Netherhells. Why, then, when he fights us, does he keep losing?"

"Simple!" a small voice chimed. "That's because he never had to fight Brownies before!"

"And, if I had my way, he'd never fight Brownies again!" Snarks snapped. "No, that is not fair. Your shoe trick was rather good. Short as you are, you did play a part in this battle." The demon rubbed thoughtfully at one of its small horns. "And I think you have given me a clue to Guxx's defeat."

"Yeah! Like the positive force of Brownie Power!"

Snarks chose to ignore the tiny voice.

"Guxx seems intent on attacking us with as large a force as he can muster at any one time. But why attack us when we were in a large group, instead of waiting until we were more isolated? The answer lies with Ebenezum."

I paused, letting the beautiful Alea go a few paces ahead. It sounded as if Snarks's Netherhells training might be strategically important after all.

"The Forxnagel is imminent," the demon continued. "The first encounter the Grand Hoohah had with the wizard Ebenezum was decisive in more ways than one. Not only did it cause your master's malady, and thus bring about this journey, but it affected Guxx as well. I believe the wizard's resilience in facing Guxx's demonic hordes has actually made the demon lord afraid. He attacks blindly, without reason, whenever he has the opportunity. Even though he has attained the Grand Hoohah, I feel that Guxx fears, as long as the wizard Ebenezum is alive, that his Forxnagel spell will never succeed!''

"Doom! So he will attack again and again?''

"Wow! It sounds like you're going to need Brownie Power even more!''

"Doom!" Hendrek repeated. "An amazing piece of conjecture. And yet, in a fiendish way, it makes sense.''

"As does everything I say,'' Snarks readily agreed. "Now perhaps you'll listen to those diet plans I've laid out for you. Not to mention a few technical pointers I can give you on handling your warclub!''

"Doom!"

"Oh, Wuntie!" Alea rubbed my shoulder gently. "Do you think we might stop and rest for a little while?''

Uncertainty stabbed me as I glanced at the young woman. Had I been driving them too hard? I asked Alea if she was tired.

"Well, of walking, yes. I'm always a little jumpy after a performance. Wuntie? I was wondering if, when we stopped, we might be able to rest a bit farther down the path from the others?''

Alea was right. We had not really had time for a serious talk since she and Hubert had dropped in among the mythological beasts. I looked at her bouncing blond curls, dark gold in the forest shadows.

Still, I pondered Snarks's words. If he was correct, the demons would not leave Ebenezum alone. What if they attacked my master and Hubert as they awaited us?

"Alas," I said reluctantly. "Alea, we have no time for that now. Our purpose is to travel as far and fast as we can. We must succeed, for Vushta, and my master!"

"Oh, Wuntie!" Alea sighed. "I love a simple man of principle!"

"Indeed," came a voice from just up the path.

With my concern over Alea's welfare, I had failed to notice that we had entered a small clearing. Some fifty feet before us was a nearly dry riverbed. And sitting on a rock at the river's edge was the wizard Ebenezum.

"Wuntvor," my master said. "If you can ask the others to wait there, I think now would be a good time to have a conference." He nodded to Alea. "Hubert is up in the air. Said he wanted to stretch his wings."

I told my master briefly about Snarks's conjectures.

"Interesting," my master replied, "and very possibly true. I knew Snarks could be a valuable addition to our party. And, if he is correct, there is even more reason for us to hurry. For, Wuntvor, we are getting close to our destination."

"Vushta?"

The wizard nodded. "I believe we have nearly traversed the entirety of this so-called Enchanted Forest. There is but one final obstacle to overcome. If my calculations are correct, this path should lead us to a fishing village on the edge of the Inland Sea. Once we are there, it should be a simple matter to book passage on a boat, and sail across the sea to Vushta!"

Vushta! I swallowed hard. With the labors of recent weeks, the word had almost lost its meaning, and I had sometimes felt it might be an unattainable dream. Now, though, I might walk in that dream, and pass down streets where, were a man not careful, he could be cursed for all eternity. It was almost beyond imagining!

Would I really get to see the thousand forbidden delights for myself?

"Hey!" a small voice called from the other side of the clearing. "Isn't it about time for another Brownie wish?"

"Indeed?" Ebenezum queried. "Are you eager for us to use them up?"

The little fellow shook his tiny head. "I just want to show you what a Brownie can do! I mean, we got one good wish going awhile ago. Since then, though, my track record hasn't been so terrific!"

I thought I detected a look of panic deep within the wizard's eyes. Perhaps the thought struck him, as it did me, that we might have a wish-attempting Brownie as a constant companion for the rest of our lives.

"Wait a moment!" I exclaimed. "What about that rain of shoes? That was a wish if I ever saw one!"

"Hey!" The Brownie brightened perceptibly. "Those shoes were a first-class wish! Okay, if you insist. Two down and one to go. But that means I have to make the last one a whopper!"

"Good work, Wuntvor," Ebenezum whispered. "I am glad the Brownie wishes are nearly over. I fear we could not survive too many more."

Someone seemed to be humming a fanfare overhead. I looked up to see Hubert rapidly descending.

"Hello, fun seekers!" the dragon called out. "Ah, I see I didn't have to go flying to find our friends. They got here quite nicely by themselves." Hubert tipped his hat at the wizard. "Oh, I did get a look at the Inland Sea. Flying as much as I do, I'm not that good at judging walking distances. Still, I don't think that village can be much more than half a day's journey away."

Only half a day? I had to restrain myself from shouting with joy. We were virtually in Vushta already!

"Indeed," Ebenezum said, and paused a minute to blow his nose. "Well, you and Alea will be on to Vushta, then."

"Exactly!" The dragon turned to the damsel. "Sorry to thrust this engagement upon you so suddenly, sweets, but I think the wizard here has a point. We're to go ahead and inform the powers that be in Vushta about Ebenezum's findings. Then, when the rest of our party reaches the city, we'll be that much further ahead of the Netherhells' plans!"

Hubert swept his top hat in a wide arc. "Just think of the kind of entrance we can make! The publicity value of this is staggering!"

Alea looked wistfully in my direction. "Oh, there was so much I meant to say to you! So much I wanted to do!" She gave me a final, tearful kiss and then ran to the dragon. "Still, when the theater calls, one must be ready. Look me up when you arrive in Vushta!"

And with that, the two of them took to the air.

Ebenezum was on his feet. "We must get to Vushta as well. Even now, I fear we may be too late."

He straightened his robes and walked eastward on the path.

TWELVE

A wizard must always know how to use words. Practice smiling as you recite the following simple exercise. First: "The spell has not worked. It is best that you get out of your house before it explodes." Second: "The spell has not worked. It is best I get out of here before you explode." And third: "The spell has not worked. Will you please pay me the rest of my retainer before your money explodes with you?" Delivering lines like these with conviction is the sign of a professional sorcerer.

—THE WIZARD FINALS: A STUDY GUIDE
EBENEZUM, GREATEST MAGICIAN IN THE WESTERN
KINGDOMS (THIRD EDITION)

"I have something for you."

Snarks held up a length of wood. It was my stout oak staff!

"Where did you get this?" I asked incredulously.

"We found it on our way to rescue you from those

creatures. It was easy to follow. There was stuff littered all over the ground."

"Yeah!" a small voice piped from the rear. "But you needed a Brownie to point it out."

I swung the staff experimentally. Its familiar weight felt good in my hands. "Wait a second. Did you use my staff in that battle?

The demon shrugged. "Well, I needed something. It would have been difficult to push my way through that bunch of animals, just to say, 'Oh, by the way, here's your staff.' Besides, I saw you'd gotten yourself a plank!"

I glanced at the patterns the sun made through the trees high overhead. I decided I would rather not think about the plank.

"Besides, I'm pretty handy with a staff myself. Got a lot of training at Heemat's place. In fact, I could give you one or two pointers—"

"Doom," Hendrek interjected. "We found this as well."

The warrior drew a crumpled pack from out of Headbasher's sack. It took me a moment to realize that it was the wizard's—the same pack that I had carried on my back for most of our journey!

"I fear most of the contents have been lost," Hendrek intoned as I opened the thing. "We picked up what was nearby, but we felt coming to your rescue was more important than a concentrated search."

It was true. Almost all the arcane paraphernalia was gone. Nothing remained but a few books and one rumpled piece of cloth.

I pulled what at first looked like a rag from the pack. It was the same dark fabric as the magician's robes, tastefully inlaid with silver moons and stars. I hastily shook it out. Yes! It was the wizard's cap!

"Master!" I called.

Ebenezum turned from where he walked, some twenty paces ahead of the rest of the party. I held up my discovery.

"Indeed?" the wizard said with one raised eyebrow.

"They found it on the way to rescue us!" I explained.

"That's right!" the Brownie cried. "The things you lost led us right to you! Brownies are very good at following trails. It comes from being compact and close to the ground! Talk about Brownie Power!"

"I'd rather not," Snarks murmured.

"You'd better watch out, or the next Brownie wish will center on you!"

"Gentlemen, please," Ebenezum called. "We can argue once we get to Vushta. Would you bring that cap to me, Wunt?"

The wizard fit the somewhat rumpled cap on top of his head. He allowed himself a smile. "Indeed, a wizard is never complete without his cap. Did our party rescue anything else?"

I told him about the pack and the stout oak staff.

"Nought but a few books?" The wizard sighed. "Well, let us hope that, if we encounter any difficulties, those worthy tomes will suffice. We are close enough to Vushta that, should luck be with us, we shall not need any of them."

He scratched at the hair beneath his hat. "I am glad for the return of the cap, nonetheless. The more you look like a wizard, Wuntvor, the more people treat you like a wizard."

The mage shifted his shoulders beneath his robes and began to walk once again toward Vushta.

"And speaking of magic," Ebenezum said, "were you ever able to reestablish contact with that young witch?"

Norei! With all the recent excitement, I'd barely had time to think about her. I shivered when I remembered her scream, and Guxx's demonic face reciting deadly poetry. Briefly, I told Ebenezum what had happened.

"So the demon is aware of the grackle spell?" the wizard mused. "Pity. Then we can no longer use it. Let us pray that the young lady has not been harmed."

Norei? Harmed? A cold chill shot from my hairline to my shoes. She wasn't like me, a bumbling apprentice who, with luck, could manage an extremely simple spell. She was a qualified young witch! I was so sure of her abilities that I never doubted she would be safe.

But I had not really considered who she was fighting. Guxx was no ordinary demon. He had almost defeated my master, the greatest wizard in all the Western Kingdoms! What hope would a mere young witch have against something as strong as that?

"Indeed," Ebenezum said, as if he could read my thoughts. "We can help her best by getting to Vushta as quickly as possible."

Yes, my master was right. It would do me no good to recriminate myself for walking with Alea when I should have been thinking of Norei. We were all due to fight in a drama much larger than our petty, everyday concerns. There was no time for grief. Action was all that mattered now.

The trees had been thinning for some time, so that we could see regular patches of sunlight here and there. The leaves whispered overhead as the wind picked up. The air smelled moist and tangy.

"Doom!" Hendrek called from behind. " 'Tis the smell of the sea!" The trees ended abruptly, and we found ourselves on a cliff. Below us was a small village, built entirely from stone. Beyond the two dozen houses was the largest body of water I had ever seen.

"Indeed," Ebenezum said. "The Inland Sea." He looked over the cliff edge. "There must be some way down from here."

"How about Brownie Power?"

"No, I think unless you can make a flying shoe—" The wizard hesitated. "Let me rephrase that. Unless you can make a flying shoe that you have tested before, I think we would be better off finding another way."

"Well, all right," the Brownie said reluctantly, "if that's the way you feel about it. Gee, a flying shoe? What a nifty idea! You sure you don't want to try it? I mean, my wishes have been pretty good about coming true." The Brownie tried on a winning smile. "Well, at least two of them have."

"Indeed." Ebenezum nodded at the others. "Hendrek, Snarks, see if you can possibly find a path, would you?"

"What about a bouncing shoe?" the Brownie asked. "If I made it big enough, we could all bounce down together!"

Snarks and Hendrek went quickly about their business.

"Doom!" Hendrek called. "There are some stairs here, cut into the rock. They curve around the edge of the cliff, but they appear to descend toward the village."

"Oh," the Brownie said, rather disappointed. "Then I don't suppose you want a climbing shoe, either. I mean, I could make one with really strong laces, which you could tie around trees and outcroppings of rock. What do you say?"

"Indeed," the wizard replied. "I feel the stairs might be faster." He walked over to the cliff edge where the large warrior stood. "Hendrek and Wuntvor will come with me. I fear that you other two must wait here for the nonce. We need to secure the use of a boat from the village below, and I suspect that, should the villagers see a demon and a Brownie in their midst, it might somewhat hamper our negotiations.''

"I have to stay up here?" Snarks asked, a look of horror on his face. He pointed at the Brownie. "With him?"

"I think it would be for the best," Ebenezum asserted.

"Don't worry," the little fellow said cheerfully. "I can relate some fascinating anecdotes from Brownie history to help pass the time. By the time the others return, you'll know just how Brownie Power came to be!"

"Doom," Snarks remarked.

"We must be off!" the wizard called. "Hendrek, lead the way. And keep your warclub at the ready, in case we encounter demonic intervention during our descent."

Hendrek nodded grimly, and led the way.

I heard the Brownie laugh as we carefully took the steps down.

"It won't be so bad! I'll tell you all about how Brownies got into the shoe business in the first place. You know, originally, we were going to make magic socks—"

Mercifully, the cliff face cut off any further noise from above.

The descent was not as bad as I had first imagined. What began as a cliff face soon became little more than a steep hill, and the steps carved from stone became a rocky path. We reached the village quickly, without a single sign of demonic intervention.

An old man sat on a stump at the edge of the village, smoking reflectively on a long, clay pipe. He nodded at us as we approached. Ebenezum took the lead.

"A good day to you, good sir," the wizard began.

The old man smiled. "Ah, it is a fine day, isn't it? I sometimes think late summer afternoons like this are a gift from the gods. It gives an old man like myself a chance to smoke quietly and contemplate the glory of the world around me. But I always talk too much. What brings fine people like yourselves to Glenfrizzle?"

"That's the name of your town then?" Ebenezum asked.

The old man nodded.

"Actually, we've come seeking advice."

The old man laughed. "Lucky for you, advice is my specialty. People come to me all the time to ask questions about farming and fishing." He puffed once on his pipe. "I've become an expert. That's what happens when you get too old to do anything else."

"Ah," the wizard said. "Then you're just the man we want to see. We are traveling to Vushta, and seek passage across the Inland Sea. Would you know where we might be able to hire a boat?"

"Well let's—" The man's face suddenly contorted. His eyes crossed and he blew smoke through his nose. "Passage? Vushta? Hire a boat?" He swallowed. His eyes uncrossed. He smiled at my master. "I have a pipe. It is fun to smoke my pipe."

The wizard frowned. "Indeed, but can you tell us where to find a boat?"

The old man waved his pipe in circles. His eyes followed the movement of the bowl. He giggled in delight.

"Boat?" he said at last. "What is a boat?"

"Indeed." Ebenezum stepped away from the old man. He glanced at me. "Perhaps we have some trouble with the local dialect." He turned back to the old gentleman and spoke slowly and distinctly. "Sir, we seek a ship to take us across the Inland Sea.''

"Ship." The old man rolled the word around on his tongue, as if trying it out. "Shipship shipship. What is a ship?"

"We need a vessel to take us to Vushta!" Ebenezum stepped away and took a deep breath. He had been shouting.

"Oh," the old man said. "What is a vushta? I have a pipe. It is a very nice pipe."

Ebenezum sneezed.

"Sorcery!" he cried. "I should have suspected. Quickly, men, we must get into the village before this foul spell spreads!"

Ebenezum took off at a run. Hendrek and I did our best to keep up with him.

We ran past a young woman carrying a small child. Ebenezum stopped abruptly. Hendrek and I stopped as soon as we could.

"Quick, woman!" the wizard said. "We desperately need your help."

The woman was quite taken aback. "Well, sir," she said after a moment's pause. "I will do what I can."

"Good," Ebenezum replied. "We must go to sea."

The woman nodded.

"Do you know," the wizard asked, "where we might hire a boat to take us to Vushta?"

" 'Tis child's play," the woman began. "Just—" Her head jerked back for a second. Her eyes crossed. "Boat? Hire? Vushta?" Her eyes uncrossed. She smiled sweetly and bit her lip. "Have you come out to play?"

"No!" Ebenezum insisted. "We must book passage to Vushta."

"Oh," the woman said. "I can't read books. What's a vushta?"

"The spell is spreading too fast!" the wizard cried. "We must hurry!"

We ran down the street until we reached the docks. A stocky fisherman sat on the edge of his boat, mending a net.

"Quick, man!" Ebenezum cried. "We need your help!"

"A wizard needs my help?" the man said. "And what can I do for you?"

"Perhaps the spell will not work if we are away from land. May we come aboard?"

"Sure, if you don't mind the company of a few fish."

The wizard stepped hastily onto the boat.

"Now, answer at once, for we must be away. We will pay you well if you take us to Vushta."

"Vushta?" the man grinned. "Well, as I said, if you don't mind—" His eyes crossed. His grin grew wider. "I have lots of fish."

"I don't care about your fish!" Ebenezum shouted. "Will you take us in your boat?"

"Sure," the fisherman said. "What's a boat?"

"It's what we're standing in," the wizard replied. "We need you to take us across the Inland Sea."

"Sure," the fisherman said. "What's a sea?"

Ebenezum shook his head. "We are too late again."

"Doom," Hendrek intoned.

The fisherman held up his net. "Look at the pretty string. I have lots of pretty string."

My master scrutinized the large warrior.

"Hendrek, have you ever piloted a boat?"

"Wait!" I interjected. "Be careful what you say." My master's last few words had given me an idea.

"Doom!" The warrior looked about warily. "What have you learned?"

"Don't you see?" I turned to Hendrek. "The spell only works when we turn to someone and ask, 'Can we hire a boat to go to Vushta?' "

"Doom," the large warrior said. "Then we shall never—" Hendrek paused. His head shook and his eyes crossed. "Boat? Vushta? Hire?" His eyes uncrossed. He smiled broadly. "Doom."

"Hendrek? Are you all right?" For a moment, I was afraid that I had inadvertently used the spell on him.

"Doom," he said again.

He sounded like his old self. Perhaps it hadn't really affected him after all.

"Doom," Hendrek repeated. "Doom de doom de doom de doom. I like to sing. Doom doom de doom."

"Indeed!" the wizard cried. "Wuntvor, speak no more! You have hit on the very thing. If I wasn't so pre-occupied, I would have thought of it before! It is a variation on Gorgelhumm's Spell of Universal Stupidity!"

"Doom," Hendrek said. "Doom de doom doom."

Ebenezum pulled thoughtfully at his beard. "We will cure Hendrek in Vushta. From this point on, Wuntvor, we must choose our words carefully."

Another boat bumped against the nearby dock.

"Quickly, Wunt!" Ebenezum urged. "But cautiously as well!" He ran toward the docked boat. I followed close behind. Hendrek meandered after us as well, play-fully bashing in portions of the dock with his warclub.

"Excuse us, sir," the wizard called.

The boatman looked at us dubiously. "Is something wrong?"

Ebenezum stopped running and tried his best to ap-pear casual. I attempted to imitate my master. Hendrek doom-de-doomed behind us.

"Actually, nothing is wrong, save that my two com-panions and I are stuck here on land, and we wish to—uh—'' My master paused and smiled. "We wish to not be on land.''

"What?'' the boatman asked. "Where would you be if you weren't on land? Do you want to walk around on the air?''

"No, no!'' Ebenezum said, still smiling. "You don't understand! You see, uh, we need to get to different land!''

"Really?'' The boatman began to unfurl his sail. "Well, I hope you enjoy the walk.''

"No!'' Ebenezum cried. He made shooing motions toward the ocean. "Can you go out?''

"Go out? I just came in.''

"No, no!'' Ebenezum waved frantically in an attempt to keep the man's attention. "Can *we* go out?''

"Out where?'' The man's eyes narrowed. "A tavern someplace, I suppose. You're not trying to get me drunk to steal my boat, are you? Those wizard's robes look pretty old and torn to me. They don't fool this old boatman for a minute. Where did you dig them up?''

"I beg your pardon!'' Ebenezum stiffened, the smile gone from his face. "I am a true wizard! These are my real wizard's robes! I have been through great hardship and adventure to reach this point. It is not my fault if you do not feel you have time to listen to a reasonable request!''

"Reasonable request?'' The boatman threw up his hands. "I haven't even heard anything that could be considered a civil question. Until you got angry, I wasn't even sure you were conversant in the common tongue! What are you, some sort of religious fanatics?''

"I beg your—'' Ebenezum paused and pulled on his beard. "That it is. We are simple pilgrims, unable to use certain words for religious reasons.'' He drew a sack of gold from inside his robes. "Fortunately, we are rich religious pilgrims, and will pay you well for your services.''

"Oh," the boatman smiled. "Why didn't you say so? Where would you like to go?"

"Well, I need you to take my two companions and me from this land to—uh—another land."

"Yes, yes?" the boatman urged. "Come on, my good man, I can't take you there if I don't know where I'm going. What land do you want to go to?"

"Indeed," Ebenezum mused. "Well, we need to go to a big city, on the other side of the—uh—water. A magic city!"

"Aha!" the boatman cried. "You want to hire my boat so I can take you across the Inland Sea to Vushta! Why, that's simple—"

The man paused and shook. His eyes crossed. "Hire? Sea? Vushta?" His eyes uncrossed. He laughed. "I like to laugh."

"Doom de doom de doom," Hendrek sang behind me.

"Doom de doom de doom," the boatman replied.

"Oh no!" I moaned. "We can't even imply that we wish to hire a boat for Vushta, can we?"

"Indeed not," Ebenezum replied. "Apparently, this spell—" The wizard paused and shivered. His eyes crossed. "Vushta? Hire? Boat?" The mage sneezed.

"Master?" I whispered.

Ebenezum turned to me, his face lit by a beatific smile.

"I am a good wizard. I have pretty robes. Indeedy!"

The wizard sneezed.

"Master!" I cried. What had I done?

"Doom de doom," Hendrek hummed. "Doom de doom."

THIRTEEN

Some people think of wizards as nothing more than men in pointy hats who like to go around turning people into toads. Nothing could be farther from the truth. Perhaps wizards should come together and agree on a saying or two to better humanize their profession; for instance, "Wizards are wonderful!" or "Take a wizard to lunch!" Yet I doubt this will ever occur, for wizards are by and large a solitary breed. Still, this should not stop you from trying to understand my profession. If you should offer, for example, to take a wizard to lunch, I imagine he would go gladly. And if you were to tell a wizard he wasn't wonderful, I'm sure he would be quite happy to turn you into a toad.

—*THE TEACHINGS OF EBENEZUM,*
VOLUME I

"Wuntvor!"

A woman's voice called to me. I turned in haste, almost losing my balance on the edge of the dock.

It was Norei.

"Beloved!" I cried, running back up the dock and onto the cobblestone street on which she stood. "I'm so glad to see you! Ebenezum, Hendrek, all the townspeople—"

"Oh, dear," she said. "You've been trying to hire a boat for Vushta, haven't you?"

"Then you know! It was—" I began to shake. I could no longer speak. What was a boat? What was a vushta? What was a hire?

"Oh, I'm sorry," Norei said. She recited a quick string of magic words. I blinked.

"—terrible." I finished my sentence and rushed into her arms.

"I had no choice! I realize it was a little severe, but I had to do some— Wuntvor, please!" she said as she disentangled herself from my embrace. "I know you're happy to see me, and I'm glad to see you, too, but, frankly, when I kiss you, all I can think about is a grackle!"

I stepped away from her, startled. What was she saying?

"That's much better. I'm afraid we have far too much to do right now to think of ourselves, anyway. Wait for this crisis to be over, Wuntvor. Then we can become reacquainted."

Yes, she was right! This was no time to think of ourselves! What about my master, and Hendrek, and the townspeople caught by the stupidity spell?

"So," the boatman asked, "just how much gold would you be willing to offer me?"

"Wait a moment!" called the stout fisherman. "The wizard has already asked me to ferry him across."

"Indeed," the wizard said levelly. "Apparently, we

can now discuss this at our leisure. If the two of you would care to quote me rates?"

"Doom," Hendrek intoned.

"Norei!" I cried happily. "You've removed the spell!"

"And why wouldn't I?" A playful smile touched her perfect lips. "It was my spell in the first place. I'm sorry I had to use such a strong one, but the demon Guxx would have blocked anything gentler. And I had to keep you from leaving without me, at any cost."

"Indeed?" the wizard said. "Would you care to tell us why?"

"I have been sent by my family to—" She paused, glancing at the two boatmen. "—to discuss certain matters of the strictest confidence. When you are finished with your negotiations, we should find a private place to talk."

"Agreed," the wizard replied, then returned to his haggling. In a few moments we had secured the services of the larger boat for half what the smaller would have cost us. The boatman, who believed he had struck an excellent bargain, smiled and said we would leave at dawn tomorrow. When the wizard began to protest the delay, the boatman threw up his hands and said he had to wait for the morning winds. If the wizard could produce the winds sooner, they could leave sooner.

Ebenezum turned to Norei. "No," he said, after a moment's pause. "I don't think my malady could abide it. Besides, we require some rest. And we have things to discuss."

Ebenezum gave the boatman a piece of gold to seal the bargain. Then Norei, Ebenezum, Hendrek and myself retired to the town's only inn.

"Doom," Hendrek said as he walked beside me.

"Doom de doom doom doom."

"Norei!" I cried. "Hendrek still feels some ill effects from your spell!"

"On the contrary," the large warrior shook his enormous, bearded head. "The spell has benefited me. I have discovered that I like to hum. Doom. Doom de doom doom."

I wondered what Snarks would think of the warrior's new hobby.

"Master?" I asked, reminded of the demon. "What should we do about the rest of our party?"

"A good question," the mage replied. "We will have Norei contact them, and tell them to meet us on the docks tomorrow morning. They may both be of use during the trials ahead. Tonight, however, I think we may need the quiet only their absence can bring."

With that, the wizard led the way into the tiny inn.

The room we entered was pleasantly dark and cool after the late summer's heat outside. Cooking smells wafted in through a door on the far side that apparently led into the kitchen. My mouth watered. I'd forgotten how much I liked good, inn-cooked food. I thought fondly of plates piled high with pork and mutton, perhaps a fresh-caught fish from the Inland Sea, even a roast fowl or two, washed down by a good, strong ale. Life at its fullest!

The innkeeper greeted us cheerfully, his hands wringing his apron. "Strangers in town? Of course. You would like dinner? Of course. Would you step this way please? We will give you our best table, of course. We treat strangers well here. My wife sometimes asks me, can you be sure with strangers? 'Of course!' I cry. Who are strangers but people just like us, only from a different place. Lania! Mugs and settings for this fine company!"

A serving wench appeared, laden with plates and cutlery. She smiled as she passed me. Quite a nice smile, actually. If I was not promised to Norei—but, there was no time for foolish thoughts. We must prepare for the last leg of our journey.

"And what would the party care for?" The innkeeper spoke to all of us, but his eyes rested on the warrior Hendrek.

"Doom," the huge fellow replied. "I need to keep up my strength. One of everything."

"Of course! Lania, help me in the kitchen!"

"Indeed," Ebenezum said once the innkeeper had disappeared. "Now that we are alone, Norei, I must know what your message is."

"Oh, yes," Norei answered quickly. "It is something my mother, grandmother and I discerned during one of our sessions of group magic. We tried to contact you immediately, but the demon Guxx had already blocked the way. Since I was youngest and could move the fastest, I was sent to tell you in person."

She sipped her ale. Her neck looked very attractive as she swallowed. How I wished I could kiss that neck! But no, for now I must abstain. There were more important things to attend to. Besides, I reasoned, perhaps it was best if I simply spent some time around her as an obviously human apprentice, as opposed to the grackle she seemed to remember all too well.

"I trust Wuntvor told you most of what we learned." She glanced at me for but an instant with her pale green eyes. I looked away, lest the fire building inside me consume me whole.

"But there was one thing I did not impart to our bravely flying grackle," Norei continued. "The Netherhells had prepared a truly devastating fate for Ebenezum, once he had set out to sea!"

At that point, the kitchen door banged open. The inn-keeper walked to our table, bearing a large platter. Lying upon that platter, and sagging slightly over the edges, was an even larger fish.

"For our honored guests, nothing but the best!" the innkeeper exclaimed. "Of course, we begin with a spe-cialty of my humble establishment, the great rainbow fish of the Inland Sea!"

Cooked, the fish's scales gleamed a dozen pale pas-tels, gray to blue, pink to purple. The colors were set off even more by the orange-and-green checkered vest the fish appeared to be wearing.

"Odd," the innkeeper said, staring at the vest. "That isn't usually a part of the preparation. Lania, what did you put on this fish?"

Hendrek reached quickly for the platter. "Doom!" he exclaimed.

The vest was quicker than Hendrek's hands. It slipped from the platter as Hendrek grabbed, and fell to the floor, where it solidified into Brax the salesdemon.

"Boy, are you guys in for it this time!" Brax cackled as it puffed on its cigar. "I don't know why I even bothered showing up. Well, you might just have the slightest chance of survival if you stock up heavily right now. And lucky for you, I'm still overstocked on some very attractive enchantments!"

Hendrek swung Headbasher out of its protective sack and across the table towards the demon. All four mugs of ale went flying.

"Doom!" Hendrek cried as Headbasher hit the floor where Brax had stood but a moment before. The warclub left a sizable crack in the flagstone.

"See here!" the innkeeper protested. "I'm always glad to welcome strangers into my inn. I feel as if I am

fairly open to differences in foreign customs. Still, there
are limits—''

Brax ran behind the innkeeper. ''Listen, I could sell
you a little something that would rid you of unwanted
guests instantly. It's a small, enchanted bog, completely
portable. Simply place it underneath unwanted company, and they're sucked into the mire! And it's hardly
used at all, comes with a few bones of extinct creatures—''

''Doom!'' Hendrek pushed the innkeeper out of the
way to get closer to the salesdemon. Brax scooted beneath the table.

The displaced innkeeper pointed at Brax with a quiv-
ering finger. ''If this creature is going to stay for dinner,
you'll have to pay for an extra place setting.''

''How about it, Hendrek?'' the salesdemon shouted
as it somersaulted gracefully over the swinging warclub.
''You're way behind in your payments. Now, with
what's going to happen, you'll probably never be able to
pay anything, ever again, if you catch my drift. How
about using that fine, almost-new warclub to knock
over what's available around here, say, a young witch or
a magician's apprentice—''

''Doom!'' Hendrek screamed. He leapt for the
demon and landed on the table, and the fish. The fish
and the table collapsed beneath his enormous weight.

The demon was panting as it ran to the other side of
the room. ''Really, I'm not doing this for *my* health. By
this time tomorrow, you folks won't have any health to
worry about. You don't stand a chance unless you stock
up with my weapons, and I mean stock up *heavily*!''

Hendrek picked himself up from where the tabletop
had met the floor. The innkeeper looked on in silent
horror.

"C'mon guys, I've got an investment here, you know. It gets harder every day for a salesdemon to make a dishonest living!"

Hendrek threw the fish at Brax.

"No, no, I'm sorry," the demon said. "It's too late to make things better by giving me little gifts. Hmm. It is tasty though. Urk!"

Distracted by the fish, Brax had not seen the flying Headbasher until the enchanted club had found its hellish mark.

"Easy terms!" The demon wobbled. "Years to pay!" The demon gasped. "Except, perhaps, in your case—" The demon popped out of existence.

"Doom!" Hendrek intoned.

"Is this what passes for table manners wherever you come from?" the innkeeper shrieked. "Of course! I let strangers into my inn, and this is the thanks I get. No, no, my wife tells me, what are strangers but people just like us, from another land. Hah! A land where people fall atop their food! Where people appear out of nowhere and offer to sell you swampland! I am never having strangers in my establishment again!"

"Indeed, my good fellow." Ebenezum pulled out his small sack of gold.

"Of course!" the innkeeper shouted. "You offer me gold! Another time, perhaps! But now, I will not be silenced! Out in the street! Strangers! Just wait until I talk to my wife!"

We left with whatever speed we could muster.

"Well," Ebenezum said as the door to the inn slammed shut behind us. "Perhaps we can sleep on the boat."

We walked back down toward the docks.

Ebenezum moved between Norei and myself. "You

were saying that you had a warning for me?"

"Yes, Guxx is very worried about your reaching Vushta. In fact, he seems to be petrified by the idea."

"Indeed?"

"Yes." Norei frowned. "Guxx feels you must be put out of the way at any cost. They have planned something at sea which you cannot possibly survive."

"I see." The wizard stroked his mustache in thought. "But if what you say is true, why then did they attack us in the forest?"

"Oh dear," Norei said with a sigh. "I'm afraid I'm to blame for that. It happened when Guxx discovered that Wuntvor and I had been talking, after the demon was sure he had effectively stopped all magical communications from reaching you. I might have been in trouble then, if the demon had not been so hysterical. As it was, though, the spells Guxx threw at me unraveled when he began to scream incoherently about conspiracies against him. I think he felt then that your sea death, sure though it would be, was not soon enough. So he mustered whatever demons he could find and attacked you immediately."

"Doom!" Hendrek said. "Snarks was right!"

"Indeed," Ebenezum said, pulling reflectively on his beard. "Still, I wonder if perhaps it would be best not to congratulate him, at least until this campaign is over?"

Hendrek nodded his head in agreement. "Doom."

The wizard turned back to Norei. "You still haven't told me; exactly what is this sure death I am supposed to meet at sea?"

"That's the problem!" Norei said, throwing out her hands in a gesture of helplessness. They were very beautiful hands. "I don't know. We couldn't find that out. Guxx discovered our spying, and the magical link vanished. But our eavesdropping did reveal one important fact! We learned the spell that would defeat whatever it was they sent against you!''

''Indeed?''

''Yes! All we know beyond that is the bringer of your death is very swift and sure, so we must use the spell the moment we see it, whatever it is.''

''And what is the spell?'' Ebenezum asked.

Norei paused for a second to concentrate.

''It is a poem of sorts,'' she began.

> *"Go, you creatures! Back down in the blue!*
> *Go, you demons! Wakka doo wakka doo!"*

''Indeed,'' the wizard agreed. ''It is fiendish enough to come from Guxx. And bound to be powerful. The rhyme scheme is better than most.''

''Doom,'' Hendrek murmured.

''No, I don't think so,'' Ebenezum replied. ''With the information Norei brought us, I think our mission has a chance.''

''Hi, there!'' a small voice piped. ''Rise and shine! The Brownie has arrived!''

''Doom,'' Hendrek mumbled, half-asleep.

''My thoughts exactly!'' Snarks cut in. ''But all is not lost. I am here as well!''

''Indeed.'' Ebenezum looked out from where he was using a sail as a blanket. ''Could you get on the boat discreetly? I'm afraid the owner has not been completely informed as to the true nature of his passengers.''

''Don't worry,'' Snarks said. ''I've come prepared.'' Once again in close proximity to the wizard, the demon was heavily cloaked. He lifted his hood over his head. ''Brrffll gllmlcch!'' he exclaimed.

"Fine," Ebenezum said. "Now Brownie, if you will hide in Snarks's pocket?"

"A Brownie? Hide?" The little fellow placed his hands defiantly on his tiny hips. "No sir! Those days are over! Brownies hold their heads up high!" He looked angrily at Snarks, who had said something indecipherable. "Well, maybe not that far aloft, but plenty high for our size!"

The wizard sighed. "I'll make it the third wish."

"But you can't! A pitiful wish like that? I'm sorry, the last wish has to be a whopper! I mean, we're making Brownie history here!"

"Indeed," the wizard said. "I wish the Brownie—"

"Stop where you are! I'm going!" The Brownie jumped into the pocket of Snarks's cloak.

"Good day, sir!" the boatman called from the shore. "I see you are here promptly, and you have brought your party. Excellent. We will be off. And I see you'll give me a hand with the sail?"

The rest of us stretched and stood. As stiff as I was from a night attempting sleep on this boat, I did not care. In another day or two, I would see Vushta!

My eyes were drawn to Norei, who had risen from where she had slept at the other end of the boat. There she was at the first light of dawn, her lovely hair in her eyes, yawning magnificently! Oh, what a lucky fellow I was to be in love with someone as fine as that!

The boatman stepped on board. "We are in luck. The weather is with us! We should make Vushta by nightfall tomorrow." He brushed past Snarks. "If you will excuse me?"

"Bllflldmmp!" Snarks answered.

"Beg pardon?" the boatman said. "Say, you're not a member of the original party, are you? You must be that fifth person the wizard said he was going to bring aboard. I don't believe we've been properly introduced."

"Indeed," the wizard interrupted. "That is the last member of the party, a religious zealot, who must, to fulfill his vows, always keep himself heavily cloaked. In addition, we all attempt not to speak with him."

"He hasn't taken a vow of silence, has he?" the boatman asked. "I mean, I just heard him talk."

"Indeed," the wizard replied. "In his sect, the vow of silence is not severe enough. He has therefore taken the ultimate oath of his religious order, the vow of incoherence."

"Kllfvrmmll!" Snarks complained.

"See what I mean?" the wizard added.

The boatman nodded, momentarily awestruck. Ebenezum instructed me to lend a hand in casting off from the dock. In situations of this sort, the wizard always said, it is better to act quickly, rather than to give anyone time to think.

In a matter of moments, we set sail. It was the first time I had ever been in a boat large enough for me and five others to stand in. And it was the first time I had ever been on an expanse of water larger than a small lake.

It was quite beautiful, watching the sun rise over the water, turning the sea pink, then red, then burnished gold. The gentle waves that broke across the ship's bow, at first disconcerting to someone new to sea travel, soon became comforting in their regularity, and the way they gently rocked our craft. It was a very pleasurable experience, actually, being out on that inland ocean at the first light of morning. Much of the comfort was taken away, however, by the grim fact that the Netherhells' fatal plan would attack us here, on this calm Inland Sea, and, indeed, that the attack might come at any moment.

FOURTEEN

Some mages balk at performing spells during an ocean voyage, preferring instead to dabble in sorcery in tiny rooms, precariously perched high atop the aerie towers that this sort of magician always seems to favor. The logic of this preference has always eluded me. After all, should something go amiss with either your spell or your relationship with your employer, just think how much easier it is to swim than it is to fly.

—THE TEACHINGS OF EBENEZUM,
VOLUME XXXVIII

Ebenezum turned to Norei and spoke in a low voice.

"Perhaps you could conjure a small wind spell? Nothing too big, something perhaps that would only slightly irritate my nose."

Norei frowned. "Well, I might be able to do something. I see problems, though. What if I'm busy with the wind spell when the Netherhells attack? It might take me awhile to disengage. And what if, by bringing about a wind, I rush us into the Netherhells' trap too fast for us to counteract it?''

"Indeed," the wizard replied. "I am so anxious to get to Vushta, I am not giving proper consideration to the consequences. Now it might be that, by producing a wind, we could outrun whatever the Netherhells will send against us. But there is no way of knowing. I think we need you, alert and about the deck, more than we need a breeze."

"What is this talk of spells?" the boatman called from his place at the tiller. "I am always glad to take a wizard on as a passenger. I do not discriminate in those areas as others do. But I draw the line at magic on my boat! I mean, this craft is almost paid for! I don't want anything to happen to it now!"

"You have nothing to fear on that account," Ebenezum called from the bow. "For the time being, we would like to stay as far away from magic as yourself!"

"Doom," Hendrek spoke to my master in a low voice. "Look at the way the seagulls gather on the horizon. Could that be part of the Netherhells' plot?"

I looked where the warrior pointed. Dozens of seagulls whirled in the distance.

"Indeed," the wizard mused. "Either that, or they're above a large school of fish. What would the Netherhells attempt? A seagull suicide spell? Too risky; you can never trust seagulls to do as instructed. They're always off looking for fish. Still, they may bear watching."

Hendrek nodded, his eyes fixed upon the whirling birds. "Doom," he murmured.

"Pardon," the boatman called. "Are you sure this is but a regular pleasure trip?"

"Certainly," Ebenezum replied. "What makes you ask that question?"

"Well, you folks act very odd for a group on a pleasure cruise. Every time I turn around, you're having a conference. Now look here, I would have to charge more if this were a business venture."

"Indeed." The mage stretched out upon his wooden seat, and scratched beneath his beard. "Oh, no, we intend nothing more than pleasure to come from our actions. After all, what else is Vushta for?"

"Quite right," the boatman replied. "Sorry to question you. The renter is always right, as they say."

"Indeed." Ebenezum turned out to look at the ocean.

"Brwnnmmpwrr!" came a muffled shout. The voice, somehow, sounded much too high to be Snarks's.

"Llgvvbrwrph!" Ah, now that was Snarks. I looked over to the middle of the deck, where the well-cloaked demon seemed to be doing an elaborate dance.

"Is something wrong?" the boatman called.

"Not at all!" Ebenezum said reassuringly. " 'Tis nothing more than a complex religious ritual. Wuntvor, could you go over to our friend and make sure his ablutions do not tangle his robes?"

I did as my master asked. As I approached the demon, I could see that most of the movement was in Snarks's pocket, the very place we had stashed the Brownie! What was happening?

I spoke quietly, through clenched teeth, to a point in the demon's robes where I imagined an ear would be:

"Don't you think you should quiet down?"

"Snnrfhm!" Snarks replied.

"Brwnprrfrffrr!" the Brownie yelled back.

"Will you control yourselves?" I whispered. "You two can argue when we get to Vushta."

"Up with—" the Brownie cried before I could stuff his head back into the pocket.

"I can take it no longer!" Snarks shouted, flinging

off his hood. "I have suffered enough! I will not have a little person inhabiting my clothes!"

"What is going on here?" the boatman demanded.

I turned around, trying to shield the struggling demon and Brownie with my body. "Please try to ignore it. 'Tis nothing but the latter stages of the religious ritual. It gets rather hectic, I'm afraid."

"It will get much more hectic if this Brownie doesn't get out of my robes and off this boat immediately!"

The little fellow popped his head out of the pocket. "Brownies come and go as they please. Let's see how Brownie Power does at making shoes out of demon leather!"

"Wait a second!" the boatman cried. "That fellow having the religious experience isn't human! And I think he has two heads!"

"Indeed," Ebenezum said. "That is very observant."

"Observant, nothing! If it's not human, it doesn't stay on my boat!"

"A moment, my good man." Ebenezum stood, fixing the owner with his best wizard's stare. "You were contracted to take the five of us to Vushta."

"Wait a moment!" The boatman shook his head violently. "You contracted for five persons! Human persons!"

"I'm afraid, my good man, I did not. I simply asked you if you could take five on a boat. Species was never discussed."

The boatman fumed. "I should have listened to my grandmother!"

"Indeed," the wizard replied. "We would probably all be far better off if we had listened to everybody."

The boatman continued as if he had not heard my master. "My aged grandmother was a wise woman. She used to say, always make your contracts in writing. She used to say, never trust a wizard until you have his gold. She used to say—"

"Indeed," Ebenezum interrupted the other's meanderings. "You know, there are certain rules that my aged grandmother told me as well. I believe one of those is apt in this situation."

The boatman blinked unhappily. "Which is?"

Ebenezum pulled back his sleeves, exposing his hands in prime conjuring position. "Never argue with a wizard."

"Oh. Yes, well, I guess you have a point. Sounds like your grandmother was every bit as wise as mine. Actually, come to think of it, mine liked to talk a bit too much. Never would shut up—"

The boatman returned to his tiller. Snarks and the Brownie seemed to have quieted as well. The prospect of being thrown bodily into the ocean had temporarily calmed their anger. I placed Snarks's hood back on his head.

"Thmmnnllf!" Snarks said.

"Doom!" Hendrek called.

The sky above us was filled with seagulls.

"Quickly, Norei!" the wizard said. "Everyone, cover your heads!"

In a high, lilting voice, the young witch cried:

"Go, you creatures! Back down in the blue!
Go, you demons! Wakka doo wakka doo!"

The seagulls continued to circle, as the boat slowly moved away from them.

"I don't think that was the Netherhells' curse," Norei remarked.

"Indeed," the wizard replied.

"What was that all about?" the boatman called.

Ebenezum rolled up his sleeves. "Do you wish to argue with a wizard?"

"Hold on, now!" the boatman said, pushing as far back against the tiller as he could manage. "It's one thing to argue with a wizard. It's another thing to send your boat, your sole means of livelihood, to sure destruction."

"In truth." The wizard paused, pulling at his beard. "We have not been totally fair with you, my good man. Our trip is serious business, and we will pay you accordingly. We will even pay for the sixth person, short though he is, who resides in the cloaked one's pocket."

Ebenezum pulled forth his bag of gold and rested it upon his palm. "You must excuse me. Sometimes my wizard's frugality gets the better of me. But we no longer have time for such petty concerns as money. I will give you a fair share of this purse, once our job is done. We must get to Vushta as soon as possible. There are demons who are trying to stop us, for they have a plan whereby the Netherhells will control the surface world. Because of this, your ship may be attacked during this crossing, although we have developed countermeasures that should be more than sufficient to protect us. I hope you understand the importance of our mission. The fate of Vushta, and the whole world, hangs in the balance."

"Oh." The boatman smiled. "Is that all? The fate of Vushta hangs upon our actions? We might be attacked by demons at any moment? Why don't I just jump off my boat now, and be done with it?"

"Doom!" Hendrek contributed. "Heed the wizard. Even I don't think our situation is that hopeless."

"I should have listened to my grandmother! She was always talking. Threw peach pits at me if I didn't listen. She was always talking, and eating peaches. Had a deadly aim with those pits, let me tell you. It's why I went to sea in the first place.'' The boatman shuddered. ''I'll end up as dinner for some demon! And my grandmother said I'd never amount to anything!''

''Indeed,'' the wizard replied. ''Fear not, friend Hendrek. The good boatman is already beginning to accept the situation. In the meantime, mayhaps there is something we can do beyond mere waiting. Wuntvor, you said there were still some books in the pack?''

I nodded, pulling the pack from where I had stashed it beneath my seat. I took out the three remaining books, reading the embossed letters on their spines aloud.

''Um,'' I said. ''Here's *Aunt Maggie's Book of Home Remedies*?''

Ebenezum nodded. ''Gift from my old mentor. We met her on our travels through a haunted valley. We helped her get rid of some ghosts and she gave me the book. Knowing her, she probably put a spell on it so I wouldn't lose it. What else have you got, Wunt?''

I looked at the two other books in my hands: *Vushta on Two Pieces of Gold a Day* and a well-worn copy of *How to Speak Dragon*. My master frowned as I told him.

Ebenezum chewed his lip. ''Disappointing, although we may be able to use the Vushta book, should we reach our destination. Who knows? Maybe Aunt Maggie's book has a recipe for seaweed tea? I fear that wits, not spells, will have to see us through the coming test.''

The wind picked up suddenly. It started to rain.

Ebenezum huddled in his tattered robes. ''Does the weather always change so quickly?''

A streak of lightning relit the darkening sky.

''Aye,'' the boatman said. ''We're subject to squalls out here on the water.'' He stared up into what was fast becoming a downpour. "Usually, though, there's more warning than this."

"Doom," Hendrek muttered. "Could it be—"

"Only one way to find out," Norei replied, and began to recite:

> *"Go, you creatures! Back down in the blue!*
> *Go, you demons! Wakka doo wakka doo!"*

The rain got heavier.

"On my grandmother's grave!" the boatman shouted over the gathering storm. "Not only do I have to navigate this boat, I have to listen to your poetry. Before, I was not sure. Now, you will have to pay me double!"

"Indeed," the wizard said. "We will pay you well enough." He stared up into the stormy sky. "Apparently, the poem wasn't appropriate."

"Doom," Hendrek said. "Will we have to use the poem on everything out here?"

"More poetry?" the boatman cried. "The fight with the Netherhells was one thing. That I can accept. But you should have warned me about the poetry. I may have to charge you triple!"

"Hey, guys!" A small form jumped out of the pocket in Snarks's robe. "You have forgotten the obvious solution. Brownie Power!"

The rain lessened overhead. The sun peaked through the clouds. There was a rainbow.

Snarks tossed his hood away from his face. "Mere coincidence." The demon sneered. "It has to be!"

"Who *are* these passengers?" the boatman complained. "The price of rental is going up by the minute!"

"You've laughed at Brownies for the last time!" the little fellow shouted at the demon. "We'll show you what Brownies are made of! Remember the Brownie Creed: We may be tiny, but we're terrific!" He began an elaborate dance.

Snarks placed a restraining hand on the Brownie's cap. "Are you sure you should do this? If something goes wrong, we'll all drown."

"There have always been naysayers who have sneered at greatness!" the Brownie cried. "Big ideas don't happen without taking big risks! I must do it, for the glory of Browniedom everywhere!"

"What is he doing?" the boatman demanded.

"I think it's called the Lindy Hop," the Brownie explained obligingly. "And boy, wait 'til you see what happens when I'm done!"

"I think it's going to happen almost immediately," Snarks retorted, looking about him for something to throw. "No Brownie's going to dump me into the ocean!" He picked up an oddly-colored oar.

"Where did that come from?" The boatman pointed at the orange-and-green checkerboard piece of wood.

"Doom!" Hendrek intoned, reaching for Headbasher.

"That's right!" The oar began speaking even before it had completely metamorphosed into Brax the salesdemon. "It is your doom, unless you act now!"

"Hendrek!" I warned. "Be careful of the bottom of the boat!" But the large warrior's club was swinging mightily, heedless of anything in its path. Wood splintered as Headbasher took a chunk out of the mast.

"This is the end!" the boatman shouted. "Why didn't I listen to my grandmother and become a tinker?"

"Wait a moment!" Brax ducked under the warclub. "I have something that just may save all of you! Then again, it may not. And heaven knows, it will cost a lot.

But, let's face it, you're going to need something really big—"

The salesdemon paused and blinked. It swallowed, hard.

"Oh no, not that," he whispered. "I have to be going. Sorry to have bothered you."

The demon blinked out of existence. Headbasher wisked through empty air. The large warrior sat down, hard.

"Doo—oof!"

"No!" Snarks cried in horror. "Not that! Even I don't deserve that!"

A hundred voices cried as one:

"It's Brownie Power!"

I looked up to see that our boat was filled, from stem to stern, with Brownies.

FIFTEEN

In a world that was totally objective and fair, size should make no difference in the worth of any individual or creature. But, then again, wizards should not have to work for a living, either.

—THE TEACHINGS OF EBENEZUM,
VOLUME XXIX

One of the small multitude jumped down from atop the tiller. The boatman stared after him, obviously in a state of shock. While most of the others were dressed more or less like our own Brownie, this one wore a cap and cloak of dark brown fur.

"You called, Tap?"

"Yes sir, Your Brownieship!" our Brownie responded.

"I don't believe it," Snarks muttered. "Tap?"

"I understand," His Brownieship intoned, "that some of this company have been giving you trouble, even, perhaps, implying things that might be detrimental to Browniekind?"

"Well, sir," Tap replied, "it's really only one of

them, and I think he's only trying to be friendly."

"Now, now," His Brownieship chided, "that's just the positive side of your essentially optimistic Brownie nature talking. From what I've heard, things are far worse than that! We Brownies have been belittled far too long! Remember the Brownie Creed: We may be short, but we stand tall!"

Snarks looked longingly over the side of the boat. "Maybe I could learn to swim."

"Ah," His Brownieship said. "So this is the perpetrator."

Snarks edged toward the bow. "Maybe I could learn to breathe underwater."

"Now, now," His Brownieship urged. "My good fellow, we don't want to hurt you. We just want to show you the positive nature of Brownie Power!"

"Maybe I should just jump," Snarks muttered. "I could always come up with a plan later."

"Come, fellows, let us entertain this newcomer with one of our inspirational cheers! What can you always use?"

"Brownie Power!" came the chorus.

"What always pays those dues?" His Brownieship continued.

"Brownie Power!" the chorus responded.

"What keeps away the blues?" His Brownieship was jumping up and down with excitement.

"Brownie Power!" The chorus was jumping as well. The boat began to rock.

"What should you always choose? No, no, fellow Brownies! Pull him back in the boat! You don't need to jump, friend demon! You'll grow to like this! That's what Brownie Power is all about!"

"Wuntvor?" Norei's hand gently touched my elbow. I turned to her, and found her face full of concern.

"I worry for your master."

I looked behind the young witch. Ebenezum sat at the farthestmost point of the bow, with his head over the side of the boat.

Of course! The sudden appearance of all these Brownies must be playing havoc with my master's malady. What kind of an apprentice was I to be watching some silly little drama when the wizard was in dire straits?

I moved quickly to my master. Kneeling by his side, I stuck my head, too, over the edge of the boat.

"Indeed," my master said as my head approached his. He appeared to be breathing quite normally. "One must be prepared for any eventuality, Wuntvor. When one has a malady such as mine, instant measures are often called for."

I asked the wizard if I should tell the Brownies to leave.

"On the contrary," Ebenezum replied. The end of his beard sent ripples through the water. "For the moment, I seem to be functioning quite well. And it occurs to me that, every time we have fought Guxx Unfufadoo and his demonic hordes, we have won because we had access to resources he could not foresee. Thus, when we fought together in the Western Woods, the demon did not take into account my sorcerous skills. In our first big battle at Heemat's Hovel, we were aided by hordes of religious seekers and a minor demigod. In our second battle, we were joined by a legion of mythological beasts. No, Wuntvor, I think the Brownies should stay around. They might be Guxx's undoing."

"See?" a small voice said in my ear. "What did I say?"

I turned to see Tap, sitting on the edge of the boat, grinning at me.

"This third Brownie wish is going to be a big one!"

Ebenezum sneezed briefly. "Wunt," the wizard said. "While I am thus indisposed, I trust you to manage the business on board. If you need me, you know where I'll be."

I nodded briefly and stood, surveying the once again clear blue sky. I looked back over to the other end of the boat. The Brownies continued their ragged cheers. Snarks was pleading with Hendrek to bash him unconscious with Headbasher. "Have you no mercy?" the demon cried.

I turned and waved our Brownie back into the boat.

"So your name is Tap?" I asked, doing my best to distract the small fellow from talking to Ebenezum.

"Yes!" Tap exclaimed cheerfully. "All Brownies are named after shoemaking noises. You know—Tip, Tap, Hammer, Buckle. We take pride in our work!"

"Wuntvor?"

I turned at the sound of my beloved's voice. She smiled in a way I hadn't seen in far too long. I forgot Tap's enthusiasm, I forgot about the boat, I forgot the impending demon attack. The world fell away, lost in Norei's eyes.

"Wuntvor?" her perfect lips said. "In all this madness, we really haven't had time to say hello. I'm afraid I've been ignoring you. We've been away from each other for so long. Our relationship before was new; we still don't know each other all that well. Yet, on my journey here, I found myself thinking about you, over and over again. Now here we are, on a ship together, awaiting imminent death. These may be our last moments together!"

"Norei," I whispered. "There's never been anyone but you." We kissed.

Norei broke it off abruptly. "If only I could get the

image of a grackle out of my head! But, Wuntvor, you really meant—''

"By my grandmother's bones!" the boatman shouted. "Something else is coming!"

I looked aloft to see what had stirred the boatman from his state of shock. Something very large was flying our way. Something very large, with a human rider and a top hat.

It was Hubert.

He landed with a gentle splash to the starboard of the boat, and tipped his hat in our direction. "Don't worry," he said. "I can float. Dragons have a lot of hot air. But, if you don't mind, Alea would like to come on board and stretch her legs."

Alea jumped nimbly from the dragon's back onto the boat.

"Doom," Hendrek inquired. "Why are you returned already from Vushta?"

"Because, alas, we never made it there," Hubert replied. "It seems that Vushta is encircled with an impenetrable fog. I had to turn back. I couldn't see to land."

"Doom," Hendrek nodded grimly. "We will have to sail into it, then."

"We will have to sail where?" the boatman cried. "Not on this boat! First, you sneak aboard nonhuman passengers! Then, we are set upon by a plague of Brownies! Next, a dragon lands next to my boat. No thank you! I'm turning around! Not on my boat, you don't."

"But we have to!" I insisted. "The fate of the world may depend upon our reaching Vushta!"

"No!" The boatman shook his head. "I hear my home port calling."

"Let me handle this," Hubert remarked. "Did you

ever consider how you would feel charbroiled?"

"Char-what?" the boatman asked. "Then again, my home port isn't calling all that loudly. You have to have some adventures in your life. That's what my aged grandmother used to say."

"Be of good cheer, boatman!" His Brownieship called. "You have nothing to fear! You have Brownie Power on your side. Tell me Brownies: What's too good to ever refuse?"

"Brownie Power!"

"And what's one way you can never lose?"

"Brownie Power!"

"And what's better than eating—"

"Oh no you don't!" Snarks screamed, startling His Brownieship midcheer. "I've had enough of this Brownie business!"

The Brownies, who had been jumping about with their Brownie Power cheers, continued leaping and shouting. But there now seemed to be an angry edge to their voices.

"Fellow Brownies!" His Brownieship called out, quieting the multitude. "We have tried Positive Brownie Action on this lost soul. But, occasionally, some of the uninformed have too many barriers to accept the simple truths that we embody as very special magical creatures. It is time, therefore, to have a reasoned dialogue! Come, sir demon! Say what you will!"

Snarks was taken aback. "You want me to talk back to you?"

"Certainly, sir!" His Brownieship replied. "Whatever you want! It's your turn now!"

"Well," the demon said tentatively, "you are rather short."

"Yes, that is undeniably true," His Brownieship

stated. "On the whole, we are much shorter than demons. An important point, well worth making."

"You're not going to disagree?" Snarks replied.

"No, no, it was a valid point."

"Well—of course it was. All my points are valid."

"Even those two at the top of your head? Sorry, just a little Brownie humor, there. I'm sure you believe in everything you say. Are there any more points you would like to make?"

"Well, maybe not." Snarks seemed rather unnerved. I had a feeling this was the first time in his demonic existence that anyone had totally agreed with him. It was a strategy diabolic enough for the Netherhells!

"See how much better things are when you have a reasoned Brownie dialogue? That's what we call Brownie Power!" His Brownieship shouted. The rest of the Brownies cheered.

Snarks retreated within his hood.

"Wuntvor?" Norei whispered. I turned to look at her large green eyes, flecked with little bits of brown. "You were saying something, before the dragon came."

"Yes, my beloved?" I replied. Was this the moment I had been hoping for, when Norei would tell me she was mine?

"Oh!" another voice called. "There you are, Wuntie!"

"Wuntie?" Norei cried in a voice much louder than a whisper.

I shook my head to try and stop the ringing in my ear. Alea stood before me.

"Uh," I began. My mind raced, trying to think of something appropriate to say.

"Hello," I managed after a minute.

"Since we had to turn back from Vushta, I thought

we could finally spend that time together—" Alea paused when she saw Norei's hand touching mine. "And who is this creature?"

I turned to Norei. She was staring at me with a look more severe than anything I had ever gotten from Ebenezum. I swallowed.

"Wuntvor?" Norei's words were clipped, as if they had been cut from her breath with knives. "Why is this woman calling you—" She paused to increase the intensity of her stare. "—Wuntie?"

"Well, um, er," I began.

Alea snorted derisively. "Wuntie, why don't you tell this newcomer what we meant to each other, back in Wizard's Woods?"

Norei gasped. "Wuntvor!" she cried. Her voice had heated considerably. "Is this true?"

"Well, er, um," I tried to explain.

"You let me waste all this time, thinking of you, building an image of the two of us together!" Norei recoiled from me in horror. "And to think I let you nuzzle me when you were a grackle!"

"A grackle?" Alea asked. "Oh, I knew a relationship with a wizard would be different! Oh, Wuntie, we could have had such fun! If only you hadn't started up with another woman the minute my back was turned!"

I had to stop this! "Well, um, that's not exactly—" I interjected.

"The minute your back was turned?" Norei repeated. "Wuntvor, you claimed but a moment ago that I was the only woman you had ever loved!"

"Wuntie!" Alea demanded. "Is this true?"

I had to say something! "Well, it is, well, I mean, but—"

How could this get any worse?

There was a noise like an earthquake beneath the boat.

No! It wasn't an earthquake. It was two hundred dancing Brownie feet!

Then there was an explosion. The boat seemed to have moved some distance.

Something huge reared its head at that spot in the ocean where we had been mere seconds before. This was the Netherhells' attack!

"Krrraakennn!" a mouth in a head the size of your average palace howled.

"Wow!" Hubert replied from above. "What an entrance!" He seemed to have taken flight about the time of the explosion.

The monster turned to regard us. It was a deep green color, close to the shade of the sea at twilight. At the moment, it pretty much took up most of the sea, anyway. Its giant, reptilian coils surrounded the boat, sending displaced water cascading across our decks.

"Yoouu moovvedd!" the huge head remarked. "Iii willl havvve tooo trryyy aaggaainnn!"

"Excuse me, you very large fellow?" The dragon shot out a spurt of flame to try to draw the monster's attention. "You are a Kraken, aren't you? Do you think we could have a little talk, reptile to reptile?"

The huge head glanced slowly up to regard the dragon. "Noooo!" it said at last. "Tiime tooo eeeeattt!"

"Come on, Brownies!" His Brownieship cried. "Time to do your stuff!"

The two hundred sets of tapping toes were at it again!

"Quick now, for Brownie Power! Let's try Plan B!"

I imagined the "B" stood for Brownie. While most of the little fellows maintained their relentless dancing rhythm, about a dozen or so split off to do some sort of alternate dance all their own.

The wizard sneezed mightily. "Norei!" he gasped. "Your counterspell!"

"Heavens, yes!" The young witch shook herself out of her shocked stupor. "Wuntvor! Join with me. We must be heard over the dancing!"

As one, we began the rhyme:

> "Go, you creatures! Back down in the blue!
> Go, you demons! Wakka doo wakka doo!"

"Hhuuhh?" the Kraken responded. "Wwellll, allll rriighttt!"

> "No, you don't, you're all at sea!
> The Kraken stays right here with me!"

It was only then that I saw the Kraken had a rider, a green hairy fellow wearing a helmet. The fellow pulled his helmet off. It was Guxx Unfufadoo!

"Geeee," the Kraken said. "Mmmaake uupp yoouuurrr mmindddss."

Guxx cried:

> "Don't worry, that spell is obsolete!
> All you should do now is eat!"

"Oooohhh," the Kraken remarked with a smile the length of your average river. "Goooddd. Mmmmmrrrrf-fflllxxxppttt."

An incredibly giant shoe had appeared to cover the Kraken's head.

The Kraken ate it.

"That's always been the problem, using that spell on

omnivores," His Brownieship admitted. "Tap! Are you ready?"

"You've got it, Your Brownieship!" The smaller group of Brownies danced with redoubled fury.

Guxx jumped up and down on the Kraken's enormous coil and screamed in our direction:

> *"I've got you now, you wizardly pest!*
> *In a Kraken's stomach you will rest!"*

The wizard, for his part, seemed to be sneezing his life away in the bow of the boat.

Norei and Alea stood to either side of me, transfixed with terror.

"Wuntvor!" Norei shouted over the furious dancing. "I don't know any spells big enough to stop that thing!"

"Wuntie!" Alea sobbed. "What can we do?"

"Well, um, er," I replied.

There was another sizable explosion.

"What's going on here?" an authoritatively grating voice shouted. "I hope whoever brought us here has some gold!"

"Pop? Look down there! I don't think we should worry about gold at a time like this!"

It was the mythological creatures! Flying above us were the Rok, the Griffin, the Hippogriff, and half a dozen more. The Brownies had brought reinforcements!

"Waaiittt aa minnuute! Arrre theeessse creeeatuurress onn theee ootheerrr ssiide?"

Guxx screamed:

> *"What does it matter? Big or small?*
> *Open your mouth and eat them all!"*

The Kraken looked down at the demon. "Nnnnoooo.
Iii knoooowwww theeeesse beeeaassstss offf aairrr annnd
sseeea! Annnd mmyyy taaaiilll isss beeeinngg womm-
bleddd! Theeyyy arrrre mmyyyy uuuunnionnn
bbrrroothherrs! Iii hhaavvee aaa carrrdd ffoorr
AFTAOMAIBAC!"

"Afteromay what?" Guxx shrieked as the Kraken's
scales began to resubmerge.

"Yoouuu dooo nnott eeeatt youuurrr uunnionn
brrotherrs!" the Kraken stated as it settled into the sea.

"Oh, no!" Guxx cried. "Wait a minute while I—"
The demon paused, its skin a pale green. There was a
note of panic in its voice. "What rhymes with helmet?"

Guxx was swallowed by the ocean depths.

The Brownies cheered as one.

"Now that—" Tap shouted, "that's what I call a
wish!"

The Griffin landed on a bare spot on the deck. "So
we meet again. We seem to have been displaced rather
abruptly from the conclusion of our meeting. We had
only managed to ratify the first fifty-seven of our
demands. All I can say is, for your sake, I hope there's
money in this!"

Hubert belly-flopped into the water. Distracted, the
Griffin turned its head.

"Now, now!" the dragon exclaimed. "Let's look at
what you've done here. Your intervention helped to prevent this very important party from getting eaten. Thus
they can now travel to Vushta and save us all! What
need have you of monetary reward? Soon, you'll have
the thanks of a grateful world."

"Oh. That's true, isn't it?" the Griffin ruminated. "I
still wouldn't mind some gold."

"We apologize for the abruptness of our spell," His
Brownieship interjected. "That's just the way we are,

I'm afraid. We Brownies like to make bold strokes, and stay right there in the center of the action. That's what we call Brownie Power!''

"Still," the Griffin mused, "this trip might not be a total waste. Tell me, friend Brownie, have you and your virtually limitless group of brothers considered the benefits of joining a union of mythological beasts?"

His Brownieship tapped his tiny foot. "We might indeed be interested, if we got the recognition we deserved. We were about to return you to your meeting. If you don't mind adding a hundred Brownies to your gathering, we'll be glad to talk!"

The Brownie's small hand briefly shook the Griffin's wing. His Brownieship turned to the others on the boat. "Tap's final wish is done. So we will say good-bye, with a final rousing cheer!"

"What small folks are making news?" His Brownieship cried.

"Brownie Power!" the others shouted back.

His Brownieship waved his tiny fists aloft. "Who's so cute you can't refuse?"

"Brownie Power!" the others cried, raising their tiny fists as well.

His Brownieship paused dramatically, took a deep breath, and shouted even louder than before:

"And who's the best at making shoes?"

"Brownie Power!"

The response was deafening.

"Next time you need to save the world, don't hesitate to call!" Tap called to us.

And the Brownies and mythological beasts were gone.

SIXTEEN

The sages put great stock in saying that every ending is truly a beginning, or every beginning an ending, or insisting that there are no endings or beginnings, or remarking that there is nothing new, and we are doomed to endlessly repeat ourselves. Or have I said all this before?

—*THE TEACHINGS OF EBENEZUM,*
VOLUME LXXXVII

"At last!" the wizard sighed. "I can breathe again!"

He blew his nose profusely on the remains of his sleeve. When he was done there was nothing but quiet. The world seemed perfectly still.

"By my grandmother's beard," the boatman swore, "the wind has died completely."

"Doom," Hendrek remarked, rebagging his enchanted warclub. "Don't you mean your grandfather?"

The boatman shook his head. "You don't know my grandmother. If there were beards to be grown in my family, she would have been the one to do it."

I looked out over the ocean. It was as if it had seen

too much action with the Kraken and the others and now needed time to rest. We were totally becalmed.

"Indeed," the wizard remarked, much recovered. "Do you have any idea how long this lack of wind will last?"

The boatman frowned. "After what has happened here today, I refuse to predict anything."

The wizard nodded. "Too true. With what has happened here today, we may have turned nature completely around." He pulled on his beard reflectively. "But we must get to Vushta at once! Norei, can you help?"

The young witch bit her lip. "I fear I lack the experience. I can think of a wind increase spell that I might be able to recite from memory. But how can I increase a wind that isn't even there?"

"Hubert!" Alea called. "You remember the big finish we used to do at the Middle Kingdoms' Summer Fair, where you would drag the house across the courtyard? Could you tow the ship as well?"

The dragon sighed deeply. "Alas! On a better day, I would give it a try. But this day has taxed all my strength and cunning. You saw my last landing. Terrible! I am deeply in need of sustenance!"

The boatman looked alarmed. I hastily assured him that the dragon would eat no one with whom he was personally acquainted.

"Doom." Hendrek pointed beyond our bow. "The fog is coming."

The large warrior was right. A cloud seemed to skim silently across the ocean, headed in our direction. It was still some distance away, but the gray tendrils looked as if they were closing upon us rapidly.

Ebenezum picked up his pack. "If only I had not lost

my library when we were captured by the Rok. When I left the Western Kingdoms, I brought a spell for every occasion." He pulled the three remaining books forth. "Now all that is left is a travel guide, a dictionary in case we wish to speak with Hubert in his native tongue, and this slim volume of household spells from my old mentor."

I thought back on our visit to Aunt Maggie, and how she had given Ebenezum a spell to sneeze his way free of death and his legion of ghosts. I remarked upon it to the wizard.

"It's too bad we don't have Aunt Maggie here to help us all over again," I added.

"Wuntvor!" The wizard jumped up so quickly that he almost fell out of the boat. "That's it!" He pounded the book in his hand. "We do have Aunt Maggie here! We adapted one of her crop increase spells to my needs, so that, instead of sneezing like a normal human being in dire distress, I would produce a superhuman sneeze! Such a sneeze is needed again!"

Quickly, the wizard told me what to look for in the book, and the slight adjustments that needed to be made. He removed his hat and placed it in his pack. He turned to the others.

"Snarks, take off your hood! Hendrek, wave that warclub about! Hubert, breathe what flame you can muster! Norei, ready your spell! And boatman, steer true, for all our lives depend on it!"

My master took a deep breath. "I must be careful to face the stern. Wuntvor! Repeat the spell of increase!"

We all did as we were told. And my master reacted magnificently.

Thus did we sneeze our way to Vushta.

*   *   *

Or so we thought. The fog thinned as we approached land, and enough of a natural breeze arose to allow Ebenezum a rest.

But Vushta was not before us. I strained to see the city of a thousand forbidden delights, but all I could discern was a series of low, brown hills.

"Indeed." Ebenezum propped himself up on his elbows from his position at the bottom of the boat. "Perhaps I have blown us off course."

"Not according to my calculations, you haven't," the boatman replied. "On my grandmother's grave, as hard as you blew, I steered this boat straight. We should see the city at any moment. That is, of course, unless Vushta has moved." The boatman laughed at his own witticism.

The fog was clearing as we approached the shore. The low, brown hills were getting clearer. And there was something behind them, something darker. Perhaps I would be able to see the towers at any second, maybe even glimpse a forbidden desire or two taking place high atop some minaret.

"Oh, Wuntie!" Alea said close to my left ear. "It is such a wonderful city. You must let me show you the sights!"

I was aware of Norei, close by my right ear. "Alas, if only you had the time, Wuntvor. I fear we will all be much too busy defeating the Netherhells. But I guess that's something actors don't have to think about!"

"They couldn't have!" Snarks cried sharply, stopping any further exchange from the women at my sides.

The fog lifted entirely, and we all saw what Snarks's sharp demon eyes had discerned a moment before.

Behind the low hills of the shoreline was a black, gaping hole.

"It's gone!" Hubert, who had done his best to swim behind us, cried.

"Indeed." Ebenezum sat up entirely. "Are you sure?"

"Of course!" the dragon cried. "It was here two weeks ago when I left! But now Vushta is gone!"

"What does this mean?" Norei asked.

"It can mean but one thing." Ebenezum pulled grimly at his beard. "The Netherhells could not prevent us from getting to Vushta. Instead, they have prevented Vushta from coming to us."

The true horror of it overwhelmed me. "You mean," I whispered, "the Netherhells have stolen Vushta?"

The wizard nodded grimly. "It is their master stroke. They have pulled the sorcerous resources of Vushta beyond our grasp." He frowned and pulled upon his beard. "Now, I fear that nothing can stop the Forxnagel!"

"Doom!" Hendrek intoned.

For once, we all feared he might be right.

THE END

(or is it?)